"The girl lay on the surface of the sea, looking into the water through a mask, and was afraid . . . she was staring at a sharp and pointed bill of bone that quivered three feet from her chest. The bill swooped back to a broadened base, and ended in two clam-size black eyes as cold as night . . ."

From the depths of the sea, the unknown killer creature rose.

From the depths of her own compulsion, the girl was drawn to meet it.

From the imagination of the most gripping storyteller of our time comes a novel of the coupling of danger and desire—and the bloodstained horror that it spawned.

THE GIRL OF THE SEA OF CORTEZ

"GREAT . . . EXCITING . . . YOU'LL READ IT AGAIN AND AGAIN"

—*Tampa Tribune*

"BENCHLEY'S BEST YET!"

—*Montgomery Advertiser-Alabama Journal*

Books by Peter Benchley

THE GIRL OF THE SEA OF CORTEZ
THE ISLAND
THE DEEP
JAWS
TIME AND A TICKET

The Girl of the Sea of Cortez

Peter Benchley

BERKLEY BOOKS, NEW YORK

This Berkley book contains the complete text of the original hardcover
edition. It has been completely reset in a typeface designed for easy
reading, and was printed from new film.

THE GIRL OF THE SEA OF CORTEZ

A Berkley Book / published by arrangement with Doubleday
& Company, Inc.

Printing History
Doubleday edition published 1982
Berkley edition / June 1983

ISBN: 0-425-06005-5

For Kate Medina

I

THE GIRL LAY on the surface of the sea, looking into the water through a mask, and was afraid.

She was surprised to feel fear—a true, deep fear that bordered on panic—for not in years had anything in the sea frightened her.

But then, never in her life had she been actively, aggressively menaced by an animal. Creatures had snapped at her, and some had circled her, hungry and curious, but always a show of strength and confidence had sent them on their way in search of more appropriate prey.

But this animal did not seem to want to bite her, or eat her. It looked to her as if it wanted simply to hurt her, to stab her.

It had appeared with magical speed. One moment the girl was gazing into an empty blue haze; the next, she was staring at a sharp and pointed bill of bone that quivered three feet from her chest. The bill swooped back to a broadened base, and ended in two clam-size black eyes as cold as night.

Unlike the other billfish, this one had no fin on its back. It had instead a dorsal sail covering most of its backbone, which could lie flat against the back and be almost invisible, or stand in proud display.

Or, when the fish was agitated, as now, the sail pulsed up and down, up and down, as the head of a serpent hypnotizes a rodent.

The fish's tail was like a honed scythe. It twitched once, a shudder passed along the body, and the bill jerked quickly, startling the girl.

She did not know what to do, how to behave. Backing away was no answer: This was not territorial aggression, for this was not a territorial animal. It cruised the deep water of the open sea; it knew no home.

To move suddenly *at* it was no answer: The fish was supremely confident of its superiority over her—in speed and strength and agility—or it would not have approached her. She could not hope to shoo it away.

And to stay where she was seemed to be no answer: Apparently, she was somehow irritating the fish, for it shook its head, and its spear sliced the water and she felt its force against her chest.

Its long, slim pectoral fins dropped; its back hunched; its tail twitched. Its entire body was a cocked spring, ready, at the release of an inner trigger, to impale her on its bill.

Why?

It could not be pure malice, for her father had taught her that malice did not exist in animals. Animals could be hungry, angry, frightened, hurt, sick, defensive, protective, jealous, careless, or playful—and in any of those states could become vicious or violent—but not malevolent.

What, then? What did it want?

Again the head shook, and the spear slit the water.

She wondered if she could make it to her boat before the fish attacked. She fluttered her fingers and toes, hoping to propel herself backward, inch by inch, closer to her boat.

But how far away was the boat?

She turned her head a half-turn, flicked her eyes over her shoulder, saw the boat, and turned immediately back to face the fish.

It was gone.

She had felt nothing, heard nothing, and now all she could see was the endless blue.

II

THERE WAS NO electricity on the island, and kerosene lamps burned with a thick, greasy smoke that made some people sick, so the old man and the girl chose to sit in a room illuminated only by the light that leaked around the edges of the covered windows. The old man kept the room dark intentionally, had put cloths over the windows, because the slashing rays of the late-afternoon sun colored the room with contrasts so sharp that they pained his eyes and confused him. He had cataracts in both eyes, and sudden bursts of bright light felt like little explosions in his brain.

The old man's name was Francisco, but everyone called him Viejo, Old Man, even the children who might have called him Grandfather or a pet name, because Viejo was an honor, a title as significant as Excellency or General. To attain old age was a true achievement.

The girl's name was Paloma—Dove—after the morn-

ing bird that cooed a prelude to the cock's crow. She
was sixteen.

"I don't understand, Viejo," she said. "Nothing like
that has ever happened to me before."

"You had never met a bad animal before. Now you
have. It had to happen, eventually."

"Forgive me, but . . ." She hesitated. "Papa always
told me there was no such thing as a bad animal."

"Your father Jobim was a . . . a curious man." Viejo
sought gentle words to describe his son-in-law, rather
than those that came quickly to mind. "Of course there
are bad animals, just as there are bad people. I am only
grateful that the sailfish you met today was not truly
bad, or he would have run you through. That happens.
Once, many years before you were born . . ."

To forestall the reminiscence, Paloma said, "I don't
see why God would create a bad animal. It doesn't make
sense."

Viejo pressed his lips together, which Paloma recognized as a sign of pique. He was a fine storyteller, and it
was one of the few pleasures that life still permitted him.

"Who says you must understand everything?" Viejo
said. "For a human being to try to fathom all of God's
works is a waste of time."

Paloma tried to retreat. "I didn't mean . . ."

"What is, is. And one of the things that is, is that
there are good things and bad things." He paused.
"They tell me you have been interfering with the fishermen again."

"No! I only . . ."

"They say you shout and make a fool of yourself."

"They can think what they please. All I did was ask
Jo and Indio and the others why they can't be more
careful. They catch everything; they bring back fish they
have no use for. They don't kill just for food. That I

could understand. The way they fish, someday there will be nothing left.''

''No. The sea is forever. And you must learn that man will hunt what he wishes for whatever reason he wishes. His judgments are his own. For example, it has been judged that some animals are good alive *and* dead, like the bonito and the tuna and the grouper. Alive, they feed other animals; dead, they feed people and still more animals, useful animals. Some animals are bad, like the sea snake and the stonefish and the scorpion. All they do is cause pain and death.

''And then there are animals both good and bad, like barracuda—which one day feeds a man handsomely and the next day poisons him—and like sharks. Sharks bring us food and money, true, but now and again they kill people.''

''What about an angelfish?'' Paloma asked. ''What could be good or bad about an angelfish? Or a pufferfish? Indio caught a pufferfish the other day, and you'd think he had caught a marlin. Why? We don't sell them. We don't eat them.''

''The fishermen make their living from the sea,'' said Viejo, ''and so they must become one with the sea and all its creatures. Sometimes, the only way to come to know a creature is to catch and kill it.''

Because Paloma did not want to distress or offend her grandfather, she did not argue further: His truths were unshakable. So, all she said was, ''Well, I hope nothing ever wants to get to know me that well.''

Outside Paloma looked to the western sky. The sun hovered over the horizon, as if about to be sucked beneath the shiny gray water.

She hurried to her rock, a narrow shelf of stone that

jutted out over the western tip of the island. She came here at this time every day, and she loved both the place and the time of day, for this was where she felt at peace, close to nature, to life.

There were a few clouds overhead, and the setting sun painted them pink, but the horizon was cloudless, a blade beneath the red fireball that was slowly sliding downward and seeming to squash oblong.

Tonight might be a night for the green flash, she thought, and she steadied her chin in her hands and forced herself not to blink as she fastened her eyes on the vanishing sun. You almost never saw the green flash: The evening had to be clear and almost chilly; no waves of heat could be shimmering up from the water; the horizon had to be sharp and without even a wisp of cloud. And, of course, you had to be there and alert, and you couldn't blink, because the green flash lasted only that tiny bit of a second as the last infinitesimal rim of sun dipped below the horizon. Many times she had missed it by blinking, and in all her life she had seen it only twice—the first time the evening long ago when her father had led her by the hand and shown her this special place.

The bottom of the sun touched the horizon, and Paloma half expected to hear a hiss as the water quenched the fire, or see a cloud of steam explode from the sea. But smoothly and without a sound, it slipped faster and faster out of the sky.

Paloma held her breath and opened her eyes as wide as she could. The last of the sun dropped away and then, as Paloma was beginning to think there would be no green flash tonight, there it was—a shining pinprick of brilliant green, gone so fast that it became a memory at almost the same instant it registered as a sight.

Paloma watched the sky for a moment more, enjoying the changes that happened with such speed only at the beginning and end of the day. The yellow light was fading, following the sun to other parts of the world. The sky overhead was darkening quickly and soon was speckled with stars, and only the faintest splash of pink still touched the clouds.

Paloma felt suddenly calm and happy. Seeing the green flash was supposed to be an omen of good fortune, and though she didn't really believe in omens, surely it was better to have seen it than not to have seen it.

She rose to her knees and was about to leave the rock when a flicker of movement made her look back at the water. What she saw made her stop and stare and catch her breath again.

Rising clear of the water, outlined against the lapis sky, twisting in a spasm of pure pleasure, was an enormous marlin. Its saber blade sliced through the air, its sickle tail arched upward, and then, in graceful slow motion, the huge body slammed down upon the water.

It was a full second before Paloma heard the heavy, resonant boom, and by then all that remained as testimony to the acrobatics was a spreading ring of ripples on the sea.

That, Paloma thought, was definitely something special. Maybe nature is telling me I *should* believe in omens.

With a feeling of privilege, of being witness to nature reveling in itself, Paloma started for home. As she walked along the path, she looked down and saw her brother, Jo, and his two friends approaching the dock in their skiff.

Paloma could see from the top of the hill that they had had a good day. The bow of their boat was heaped high with fish, a kaleidoscope of glistening colors in the fading light. And Paloma could see, even from where she stood, that they had taken fish indiscriminately: Whatever they could catch they had killed. There were angelfish and rockfish, bonitos and jacks, pufferfish and stingrays, and even one of the rare and strange and furtive creatures called guitar sharks—harmless and, to fishermen, useless. Those fish that would not take a hook had been harpooned. Those that had eluded the harpoon had been netted.

As Paloma watched, Jo shut off the outboard motor and guided the wallowing skiff toward the dock, while his mates culled the piles of dead fish with their fingers, throwing overboard those that were not worth selling.

When Paloma had first seen them do this, she had erupted in fury, screaming at Jo, demanding to know why, if they intended to throw back the fish, they didn't do so as soon as they caught them, when the fish still had a chance to live.

If Jo had been startled at her anger, he had nevertheless been forthright in his response. "Early in the day, before we know the size of the catch, any fish is a good fish. By the end of the day, if the catch has been rich we can afford to keep only the good ones. So then we throw the bad ones back."

Paloma had tried to argue, but Jo had walked away, saying that was the way things had always been, and that was the way they would remain.

Now, she watched as the one called Indio picked up a small fish by its eye sockets and waved it at the other mate, Manolo. Though she was still a distance from them and the twilight was deepening, she could tell them apart by the color of their hair. Indio always wore a hat on the boat, so his hair had remained black. Manolo kept his head cool by pouring salt water on it, so his hair had been bleached to a light brown, just as Paloma's own long auburn hair had been bleached nearly blond by salt and sun. Indio said something now and threw the fish at Manolo, who picked up another fish by its tail and whacked Indio on the head with it.

Yowling and cursing, the fishermen flung fish at one another. Most missed their targets and landed in the water, to float there belly up.

To Paloma, striding down the hill, the fight was nauseating, the waste obscene. It offended something deep inside her to see dead animals treated as if they had never been live beings.

She bent over and picked up a rock and called out, "Hey!" The three in the skiff looked up. "If you have to throw things at each other, throw these." And she cocked her arm and threw the rock as hard as she could, hoping it would strike the skiff and knock a hole in it. But the rock flew wide and plopped in the water, and Jo responded by laughing and ticking his thumbnail off his front teeth and pointing at her—the coarsest, most insulting, and most contemptuous gesture he could make.

Paloma turned away.

Her father had explained the problem to her many times, during those early days when she had first complained about the young men who fished without care, taking everything and wasting much. "The sea, this sea, is too rich," he had said. "It has too much life."

She had not understood.

"If fish were in short supply here, fishermen might fish with care, in self-defense, for fear of killing off their livelihood. But here," Papa said, "nature seems to be showing off, proving to us how rich it can be. There is so much here, people see no reason to be careful. One day they will, but by then it may be too late. For now, it is all there to take."

Paloma had loved the sea since the time of her earliest memories. Her father, Jobim, had recognized the affinity between his first-born child and the sea, and had determined to nourish it. When she was a baby, he had bathed her in the sea and taught her to float, and then to swim, and to fear few living things but to respect them all.

And he had captivated her with his descriptions of the things that made their sea, the Sea of Cortez, unique.

The Sea of Cortez itself, he said, existed because of an ancient accident. Ages and ages ago, the peninsula known as Baja California had been part of the Mexican mainland. Then, at some point in prehistory, the plates that fit together to make the earth's surface had realigned themselves and caused what must have been the most spectacular earthquake of all time.

"You know how you take an old, ratty shirt and tear it up the back to make rags?" Jobim had said. "That's what happened to Mexico. It split along its main seam, the San Andreas Fault. And when the seam split there was a big space, and the Pacific Ocean rushed in, and a new sea was born."

The sea had had no name then, of course. Jobim read to her from a book that said it was not until 1536 that the sea was named for the Spanish explorer Hernando Cortez, who discovered Lower California and the sea that separated it from the Mexican mainland.

"Isn't that funny?" he had said. "Doesn't that make you laugh?"

"What?" Paloma wanted very much to share the laugh, but she didn't understand. "What's funny?"

"That they say some Spaniard discovered this place. Your ancestors were here, living and farming and fishing, when the Spaniards were still living in caves and eating bugs. All Cortez did was kill people and go on his way." Papa shook his head. "And for that they named the sea after him."

One book even credited Cortez with naming all of California. According to the story, as they cruised north along the west coast of the American continent, the Spaniards suffered badly from the heat. At one point, Cortez was supposed to have remarked, in Latin, to one of his officers that he found the region to be stinking hot, as hot (*calidus*) as a furnace (*fornax*).

"Nowadays," Jobim had said, "some people don't call it a sea anymore. They call it a gulf, the Gulf of California. But it doesn't need a name. It is the sea. There are three things that make up life here: the sea, the land, and the people. They don't need names to separate them." He had smiled. "If you can't tell the difference, life won't be easy for you."

So to Paloma, it was, simply, the sea—provider and friend but also tormentor and enemy. For if it gave her most of what she loved in life, it had also taken from her the one thing that she had cherished most in life.

Because of its peculiar combination of mountains and water, extreme dryness and extreme humidity, Pacific Ocean winds and high sierra winds, the Sea of Cortez was a breeding ground for sudden, violent low-pressure weather systems. With no warning at all, a fine day on the sea could turn mean. Over the horizon would race a black swirl of clouds. Beneath and before the clouds, the calm sea would begin to churn. At first, there would be a sound like a distant whisper, but soon it would swell into a horrid, wailing roar.

They were called *chubascos*, and unlike hurricanes and typhoons, they did not come from anywhere: They were created right there, and they lived and died right there. So, even if you had a radio, you could not hear a weather forecast about a *chubasco* approaching.

If you were lucky and were on land, you could fling yourself into a ditch or into the lee of a hill.

If you were unlucky and were on the water, you hoped to be able to notice a few early signs—even one sign, like a subtle shift in the wind or the sudden formation of a tower of black clouds—that would give you time to run for a lee or, at least, to reach open water, where you could face the pounding waves without fear of being driven onto a rocky shore.

If you were so unlucky as to be underwater when the first signs formed, and did not see them until the storm had made up and was almost upon you, and were forced to scramble aboard your boat and start your motor and free your anchor—then all that was left to you was prayer. Sometimes it worked; sometimes it didn't.

Two summers before, after the terrible "*chubasco* of the full moon"—the moon was full and the tides were very high, which meant that the storm-driven water rose higher and did more damage—he was found, drowned, washed up on the beach of a nearby island.

That was one reason Paloma tended to question the acceptance, by Viejo and others, that everything mysterious was somehow an integral part of God's master plan.

If anyone or any thing or any force had deliberately willed or caused her father's death, that something would be the focus of her hatred till the day she died. She believed, rather, that Papa's death was an accident, a random blow, something that nothing had ordained or could have prevented. She had conditioned her mind not to think beyond that, about what might lie behind randomness or luck.

• • •

At supper that evening, Jo insisted on describing in detail, for Paloma and their mother, each of the triumphs of his day at sea.

He boasted about how many fish they had caught, about how hard the grouper had fought, about how sharks had swarmed around his boat and tried to steal his catch.

Paloma sat silently, knowing that for her to comment could lead only to argument. But Miranda, their mother, smiled and nodded and said, "That's nice."

With a glance at Paloma, Jo said, "I even threw my iron at a manta ray, a giant devilfish. He dodged at the last second and I missed. But then—I swear—he turned and attacked the boat. It's a good thing I was quick, or I would've been rammed and sunk."

Paloma said quietly, "Manta rays don't attack boats."

"*This* one did. This was a real devilfish. I swear."

"Why do you want to harpoon a manta ray? They don't hurt anybody."

"So *you* say! The devilfish is evil! That's why he has horns. He brings the face of evil to the earth."

Paloma said nothing, making a conscious effort to look only at her bowl of fish soup. But she could not resist—it came almost as a reflex—shaking her head as Papa used to, in a way that manifested contempt.

Jo knew the gesture, recognized its origin, and hated it. And so he started to shout. "What do you know? You think you know so much. You don't know anything! The devilfish is evil. Everybody knows that. Everybody but you. You don't know anything."

Miranda recognized the gesture, too, and could see in it Jobim and the conflict he had unknowingly built up between his children. Frightened, she said, "It's possible, Paloma. It could be.''

Without looking up from her soup, Paloma said, "No, Mama.''

"Don't listen to her,'' said Jo. "She doesn't know!'' He spat toward the fireplace, the way the men of the island did to show that they had won an argument.

"You may think you know, Paloma,'' Miranda said, still hoping to mediate, to placate both her children, to restore peace to the household. "I know there are times when I think I know something, when maybe I just . . .''

"Mama.'' Paloma wanted to stop Miranda's compassionate rambling. "Let's leave it.''

For a moment, the room was silent.

Then Paloma raised her eyes and looked into the taut, flushed face of her brother. The arteries on either side of his neck looked as thick as hawsers, and she imagined that she could see them throbbing. His jaws twitched, and his arm—as big around as one of Paloma's thighs—trembled.

She had wanted to avoid enraging Jo by arguing, and instead had enraged him by being silent—a silence that he interpreted as condescension.

Paloma tried to appear completely calm, confident. She hoped that her eyes did not betray her. She knew for sure that if ever he was driven to act out one of the inner tumults that tortured him, and if she happened to be the object of his fury, he could take her apart as easily as he dismantled one of the engines he so loved to tinker with.

Jo was fifteen, seventeen months younger than Paloma, yet he had the physique of a fully developed adult. From hauling lines and nets since he was a young boy, he had developed massive shoulders and arms. He could not wear a standard shirt, for the muscles in his chest and back burst the seams. From balancing in a tipping boat day after day, his calves and thighs were lined with sinews as tough as wire leader. He was short—five feet six—which suited working in boats, for a low center of gravity made quick, efficient movement easy.

A stranger would not have guessed that Paloma and Jo were siblings, or even distant cousins. She was as lithe as he was compact. She was five feet eight inches tall, and though she had not been weighed in several years, she thought that she weighed about 120 pounds. While Jo looked very much of his people—dark of skin and hair and eyes—she did not. Everything about her was light, from her bones to her skin to her hair, for she was not so much of her people as of her father.

And there, she knew, lay the core of the problem between them. Jo felt that it should be he, not she, who was more like their father. After all, was he not a male? Was his name not made from Jobim's? And yet every day, what she said, what she did, her entire manner reminded him of how close Paloma had been to Papa and how far—worse, how increasingly far—he himself had been.

Perhaps worst of all, they both knew that Jo had had a chance to be the one close to Papa. When Paloma was feeling kindly toward Jo, she acknowledged to herself that it would have taken a superhuman boy to be the son Papa wanted. What she was less eager to acknowledge was that she, a girl and a kind of son-by-default, had been taught more patiently, forgiven more kindly, praised more freely.

But once the core of enmity had been established between them, almost every other aspect of their relationship seemed to provide new antagonism. There was, for example, Jo's assumption that upon the death of his father he should become head of the family, an assumption shaken by his knowledge that, while physically capable of almost anything, emotionally he was barely able to take care of himself.

Without another word, Jo rose from the table, turned and left the room.

Miranda looked after him. When he had gone, she turned back and said, "Paloma . . ."

"I know, Mama. I know."

III

FIRST THERE WAS only one, rolling and bucking with the grace and precision of a carousel horse, exhaling a wheezy spray through the hole atop its head, its dorsal fin and glossy back shining in the low morning sun.

It crossed in front of her bow, then leaped clear of the water and dived and passed under the boat and rolled again in front.

Then came another, and another, until there were a dozen, and then a score, and then more than she could count.

They crisscrossed ahead of her boat, four and five and six in phalanx, threading together like fingers, then dispersing, to be replaced by other phalanxes on other tacks.

She paddled on, and they came from the rear, leaping along both sides of her boat, as if urging her to gather speed so her boat would make a bow wave for them to ride. But she could make no more than a ripple in the water, so they soared away off to the sides and, in the clicks and chirrups and whistles she could hear clearly, seemed to discuss what game next to play.

They charged her boat in ranks of six and dived beneath it and surfaced on the other side, and in each rank one, only one, would leap *over* the boat, over her, and as its shadow passed it rained droplets on her head.

She laughed and tried with her voice to duplicate the dolphins' chirruping sounds, in faint hope that they would think her one of them and would stay with her. But on some secret signal they ceased their frolicking and faced in a common direction and bounded off across the sea.

Paloma stopped paddling, and watched, thrilled. She felt as if she had been anointed by the dolphins: They had chosen her as their playmate in an interlude in their travels.

It was an omen, like seeing the green flash and the jumping marlin. Perhaps today would be a special day.

As usual, Paloma had awakened just before daybreak, when the sun was sending its first gray messengers into the blackness of the eastern sky. She splashed water on her face and crept out of the house and trotted along a path to a tor on the cliffs that faced the east.

To most of the islanders, the tor was a pile of rocks, nothing more. From time to time when one of them needed a boulder of a particular size or shape, he could come and take one from the tor, so by now the pile that had once been symmetrical looked like rubble.

But Viejo had told Paloma that the tor was an ancient burial mound—not for their direct ancestors, but for those who had existed back beyond memory. Once, years ago, some scientists had come up from La Paz and sought permission to dig beneath the tor, but the islanders had refused to give consent, and the scientists had gone away.

"I was young, and eager to see what was under the stones," Viejo had said, "but the elders said no, and they were right. We believed that the dead beneath the tor looked after us, protected us from something—from what, was a personal matter for each of us. So to let anyone dig it up could only hurt us. If there were bodies under there and if we disturbed them, that could only be bad for all of us. If there were no bodies, our beliefs would then seem wrong, and our faith would be shaken. So we sent the scientists away, grumbling."

The scientists did, however, leave behind them one small bit of lore which Paloma appreciated. The reason they were confident that the tor was a burial mound, they said, was its location—on the highest point on the easternmost tip of the island. Many ancient peoples believed that they had to be buried facing eastward so they could see the rising sun and benefit from its light. The cruelest thing one could do to a person was to bury him facing westward, for the poor unfortunate was condemned forever to chase the setting sun in search of light.

Knowing this, and more than half believing it, Paloma liked to think that she shared the dawn with the souls of those beneath the tor—especially with her father, who, at his request, had been buried at sea but who also, at Paloma's insistence, had been buried at the moment of daybreak and facing the rising sun.

Slowly the gray sky was suffused with orange, and then the first shimmering line of fire slipped over the lip of the world.

Paloma sat and watched the sea and tried to envision all the things that were happening below the flat, calm surface. She wished she could watch day break from underwater, for Jobim had told her that it was the time of most activity in the sea, of movement, change, and feeding.

This was true in all seas, he had said, but particularly true in the Sea of Cortez, because here everything seemed to happen at once and in the same places. As an indirect result of the same tremor that had ripped the shirt of Mexico and created the sea, deep-water fish fed in shallow water, animals that normally never saw light were swept up into bright sunlight, and the whole bustle of the sea was concentrated in a few areas. These areas were called seamounts.

Jobim's knowledge of geology had come from his elders, and from scraps of information gleaned from scientists who stopped occasionally at Santa Maria to study shark specimens. His explanations to Paloma were simple and direct.

Thousands—perhaps millions—of years after the earthquake that created the sea, other shocks and tremors occurred and caused volcanoes to heave up and erupt and, later, to collapse into the sea. Over the ages, some of them had melded back into the sea bottom, but others remained as seamounts—mountains that rose thousands of feet from the bottom of the sea bed to within fifty or sixty feet of the surface.

The seamounts were a major contributor to the abundance of life in the Sea of Cortez, for they created a kind of natural banquet that attracted animals of every species imaginable.

Deep-water currents that flowed along the bottom of the sea would strike a seamount and create an "upwelling"—the water would rush upward, carrying with it all the microscopic animals (plankton and tiny shrimps and thousands of other creatures) on which larger animals feed. The larger animals would chase their food into shallower water, and they, in turn, would be pursued by the still larger animals that fed on them.

So around a seamount, nature's whole food chain flourished. "You'll see everything, Paloma," Jobim had said before he had taken her diving on a seamount. "Little tiny things that eat great big things, and monsters that eat tiny things; critters that eat plants and critters that eat each other and critters with teeth and critters with filters instead of teeth. And the wonder is, they all get along—even though getting along includes eating one another now and then."

Now Paloma saw it every day—nature's display, its spectacular bazaar—and it was always different.

Jobim had eventually introduced her to a seamount all her own, one never visited by the fishermen because they didn't know it existed. There, only an hour's paddle from Santa Maria Island, she could spend her days watching and swimming with and, in her fancies, imagining herself to be part of, a rich undersea life.

Each morning after breakfast, she walked down to the dock. She pretended to be there to run errands for the fishermen as they prepared for the day's journey; in fact, she was there to see them off, to make sure they left before she did, so there would be no chance they could follow her and discover her private place: In a single morning's fishing they could damage the delicate balance established by nature over countless years.

Jo and the others would never discover Paloma's seamount on their own, for, like almost all the islanders, they adhered strictly to the ancient habits and traditions. They fished the shoals that had always been fished. They did not seek new grounds, and seldom changed their locations by more than a few hundred yards.

One reason they had always confined themselves to the old grounds was that they had never had a need to move: The fishing was always fine, the grounds still yielded well. True, some species—especially the territorial ones, such as groupers—were growing scarce. But if you had a big enough boat, you could balance the marketability of your catch, making up in volume what you lost in quality.

A more compelling reason for staying on the familiar grounds was that Jo and the others had no way of finding new places. He had no depth-finder that could locate a seamount, no electronic fish-finder that would allow him to chase the big schools of jacks. And it would never have occurred to any of them to let themselves be towed behind a boat in the open sea, wearing a face mask so they could spot a seamount from the surface.

They spent their time *on* the sea, never under it; none of the island fishermen stuck his face underwater if he could avoid it. They claimed to know how to swim, but most disliked swimming and weren't good at it and went into the water only by accident.

Jo had tried, when Jobim was alive, but he had hated it. From the time when he was eighteen months old and Jobim had pitched him in the water off the dock and told him to swim, he had hated it. It was alien to him, and frightening. He believed there were creatures that wanted to eat him, and that if he was not continually vigilant, the sea itself would consume him. Jobim explained things to him, taught him, cajoled him, bellowed at him—hoping that his son would be different from all the other sons, hoping that through conditioning he could overcome this strange aversion to the place where man was born. But, finally, Jobim had despaired of him, and had turned to Paloma, who did not have to try. For swimming was as natural to her as breathing, and the more he taught her the more she begged to learn.

Of course, the others considered Paloma strange, because no matter where or as what man may have originated, he was a land animal now and there was no practical purpose in putting anything into the sea except a hook or a net.

Paloma did not understand how they could live on the edge of an undiscovered world and have no curiosity about exploring it. Beneath their feet were wonders too exotic for them even to dream of. Secretly, she was glad that they left it all to her.

This morning, Paloma had tried to be more helpful than usual, to send Jo a message of truce. She did not enjoy hurting him. Besides, his foul humors made their mother tense, and when Miranda was tense, the whole house was, too.

But Jo wanted no part of a truce today. He rejected all Paloma's offers of help. When his gear and his mates were aboard, he yanked sharply on the cord of the outboard motor. The cord came off in his hand. Paloma did not laugh, but stood by and tried to appear sympathetic as Jo, for once, restrained himself, rewound the cord, pulled it, and started the motor. Paloma cast off the bow line; Jo pointed the boat toward the rising sun and, squinting, set out for the fishing grounds.

In the old days, the fishermen had fished exclusively for sharks, for one or two sharks could bring the same revenue as hundreds of other fish. The sharks' fins were sold for soup, the meat for food, the liver for vitamins, the hide for leather and abrasives.

But synthetics had cut down the value of a shark by more than three quarters. Now the massive liver was useless because synthetic vitamins had replaced liver oil. The hides brought practically no money; man-made abrasives were cheaper and just as effective and other leathers were easier to cut and process. The fins could still be sold in the Orient, and tourists bought an occasional shark jaw, and a few people would eat shark steaks or shark hash if they couldn't afford something else. But, in general, shark fishing was no longer worthwhile.

So most sharks were taken by accident, when they bit a hook intended to attract something else or wound themselves up in a net, and the fishermen concentrated on the more readily marketable food fish.

Jo and Indio and Manolo would start the day fishing with hand lines. Periodically, they would look through a glass-bottom bucket to see if any big schools were in the neighborhood. If the school fish were there, they would set their net and wait and then gather it, spilling masses of fish into their boat.

If the big boat from La Paz was due that night or the next morning, the fish would be kept cool until they could be dumped into the boat's ice-hold. If the boat was not due for a few days, the fish would have to be gutted and put on ice on the island, or they would spoil before the boat arrived.

The islanders were at the mercy of the captain of the boat. He told them the price fish would bring in La Paz and the price he would pay them per pound, and they had no choice but to accept his price. But he was not an overly greedy man, and in some rare times when the market was glutted he was known to have paid the islanders too high a price, so they could continue to buy fuel and fruit and vegetables and clothing, and thus there were few serious complaints about him.

Since Paloma was not a fisherman, and not a man, and had no official status in the community, she was not permitted to take up dock space for her little boat. She kept it beneath the dock, where it was out of the way.

When she judged that Jo's boat had traveled a safe distance, she lay on the dock and reached beneath it and pulled out her pirogue. It was eight feet long and two feet wide and, basically, nothing more than a hollow log. It was Paloma's dearest possession.

Her father had made it for her thirteenth birthday. He had ordered the log from La Paz, for there were no trees on Santa Maria, and it had arrived on the boat that came to take away the fish. Then he had built a fire on the log and burned a cavity in it, then attacked it with a chisel and a wooden mallet. Finally, he used coarse dried sharkskin to smooth the wood and erase the splinters.

And all the while he had worked on it, he had never told Paloma who it was for. She had assumed it was for Jo, and she envied him the fun he would have, the places he would go, the things he would learn.

She underestimated her father. When he gave her the pirogue, he said only, "This will give you good times."

This morning, she had tossed a broad-brim hat into the pirogue; later, around midday, when the sun was highest and the temperature over a hundred degrees, to spend more than a few minutes on the water without a hat was to invite a pounding headache and nausea. She had checked her mesh bag to make sure she had all her equipment: her face mask and flippers, a snorkel tube for breathing, her knife—a razor-sharp, double-edged blade of stainless steel with a rubber hilt—and a mango for her lunch.

She carried the knife not to defend herself against an

animal—before yesterday's encounter with the testy
sailfish she had never felt menaced by anything under
the water, and she reasoned that if a shark was going to
bite her it would move so fast that a knife wouldn't do
any good.

The knife was more a tool than a weapon. Its primary
use was to pry oysters free from the rocks on the seamount and to open them in her pirogue. Its less common but more important use was precautionary. Over
the years, fishermen had lost a lot of monofilament
fishing line. Made of nylon, the line did not degrade in
water; colorless, it was almost impossible to see underwater. The skeins of line gathered in and around the
rocks. Invisible, very strong, anchored to boulders,
monofilament line was a trap that could kill a person in
a few minutes. If a hand or a foot became entangled,
she could not hold her breath long enough to strip away
every thread and wiggle free. She would have to slash
her way out.

Paloma untied the pirogue from the dock and stepped
in. Immediately she dropped to her knees, to keep the
boat steady. She dipped the double-bladed kayak
paddle into the still water, back-paddled away from the
dock and turned west.

Now, as the last of the dolphins leaped away out of sight
toward the horizon, Paloma looked around to reorient
herself in the open sea, then dug her paddle into the
water and continued toward the seamount.

The highest point on the seamount was not in shallow
water—nowhere did it come closer to the surface than
forty-five or fifty feet—so she could not see it from her
boat. Nor could she hope to find it by timing her journey from the dock, for each day the winds and currents

varied a bit from the day before. If the tide was with her, the trip would take less time; if against her, more time; if the tide was with her but the wind was against her, the sea would be rough and hard to paddle into. A difference of five or ten minutes could mean that she would miss the seamount entirely, for its summit was less than an acre around. So Jobim had taught her to locate the seamount by using landmarks.

A few miles to the west there was an island, and on the island grew giant cactus plants. From a distance it appeared that at the very highest point of the island was a particularly tall, thick cactus. But as Paloma paddled closer to the island, her perspective on the cactus would change, and soon she would see that it was not one but two cacti. When she could barely discern a sliver of sky between the two plants, she knew she was on target.

Still, the cactus plants told her only that she had come far enough westward. The wind or the current might have taken her too far north or south. The top of the seamount was a rough oblong that faced east and west, so that its north-south contour was narrower and easy to miss. She had to locate a second landmark that would tell her her north-south position.

As soon as she saw blue sky between the cactus plants, she shifted her gaze to a fisherman's shack at the end of a point of land on a neighboring island. If she was too far north, the shack appeared to be far inland; too far south, it seemed to be floating on the water, disconnected from the land. When the shack was precisely on the point, she knew she was directly over the seamount.

She tossed her anchor overboard and let the rope slip through her fingers. Her "anchor" was nothing but an old rusty piece of iron, called a killick, but it held the small boat as well as a proper anchor would have. And it was expendable. Anchors tended to get caught in the deep crevices in the rocks of the seamount—often in water far too deep for a swimmer to reach them—and then they had to be cut away. Paloma could not have afforded to replace a steel anchor, but there was always another piece of rusted metal to be scavenged.

When the killick had set and Paloma had tied the rope to a cleat on the bow of the pirogue, she dipped her face mask in the water, then spat in it and rubbed the spittle around with her fingertips to keep the glass from fogging (not even her father had been able to explain to her why spit kept glass from fogging, but it worked); then she rinsed it again in salt water. She fit her knife down the back of her rope belt, slipped her feet into her flippers, adjusted the snorkel tube in the mask strap and, with as little splash as possible, slid over the side.

She kicked gently along the side of the boat until she reached the anchor line. There she paused, looking down through a blue haze streaked with butter-yellow shafts of sunlight, eager for the surprise that always came with the day's first glimpse of life on the seamount.

Sometimes she thought of herself as a sudden, welcome arrival at a big party, where the hundreds of regulars would silently accept her into their midst. Certainly she felt more kinship with the animals of the seamount than with most of the people on Santa Maria, for here all relationships were direct, uncomplicated, trusting.

Usually, though, such fancies embarrassed her, and she swept them from her mind, for Jobim had told her time and again not to think of animals as human beings, not to attribute to them impossible human characteristics, but to regard and respect them as entirely different creatures. Still, once in a while she indulged herself in childish fantasies.

Some days she would see a sailfish, some days a shark, some days a porpoise or a pilot whale. Some days, like today, she saw nothing but haze, for the water was not clear, made dim and murky by vast clouds of plankton and other microscopic animals driven up from the deep. She could see the top of the seamount, a rough plain of rocks and corals, and she could make out the shadowy movement of large animals. But it was all vague and misty.

If nothing would come to the surface, and if she couldn't see well enough from the surface, she had only one choice: She would go down to the bottom.

Most of the islanders, knowing little about swimming, knew even less about diving and virtually nothing about preparing for a long breath-hold descent into the sea. Paloma's training had come from Jobim, who had taken her down in stages of five feet, teaching her how to prepare for each depth, how each depth felt different in her lungs, how to avoid panic. And her training had come as well from four years of practice, and from instinct. She did not think of herself as a good diver, or a not-good diver. She knew only that she could hold her breath long enough to dive to the top of the seamount and spend enough time underwater to have fun—and return to the surface to dive again.

Lying on the water, face down, with her snorkel poking up behind her head, she took half a dozen deep breaths, each one expanding her lungs farther than the one before. After the last breath, she inhaled until she felt she was about to burst, clamped her mouth shut and dived for the bottom. She pulled herself hand over hand down the anchor line and pushed herself with powerful, smooth strokes of her flippers. As she plunged downward, she let little spurts of bubble escape from her mouth, until the feeling in her lungs was comfortable.

She reached the bottom in a few seconds and, to keep herself from floating upward, wrapped her knees around a rock. She felt good, relaxed, her lungs pleasantly full. Time had a way of expanding underwater. She might be able to stay down for only a minute and a half, perhaps two minutes, but because every one of her senses was alert, every sound and sight and feeling registered sharply on her brain. On the surface, two minutes could pass without her noticing anything; down here, everything was an experience, so two minutes could seem as full as an hour.

For the first seconds after her descent, the animals of the seamount retreated, wary of any disturbance in the water and quick to distance themselves from it. Now they began to return, as if accepting Paloma as part of life.

Something slammed her from behind, knocking her forward. She clutched at her rock perch and spun around, one arm up by her face. For a split second, she couldn't see through the cloud of bubbles. If a shark had bumped her, as sometimes they did to test for prey, it would strike again and she would be dead. Whatever it was had not been an accident; accidental collisions underwater were as rare as straight lines in nature.

Arm up, squinting through her bubbles, fighting to suppress panic, Paloma found herself face to face with her assailant. And she laughed into her snorkel.

It was a big grouper—three or four feet long, thirty or thirty-five pounds—and it hovered a foot from her face, its lower jaw pouting out from under the upper, its round eyes staring straight at her, waiting impatiently for her to do what it assumed she had come to do—feed it.

She had fed it often before. There was no mistaking this grouper: It was the only one of its size on this seamount, and it had prominent scars behind one of its gills, mementos of long-ago narrow escapes from larger predators. Sometimes she brought it bread, which it ate contemptuously, as if doing her a favor; sometimes bits of meat or fish scraps from the dock, which it gobbled up. And sometimes she forgot to bring it anything.

She had resisted giving it a human name, but she could not resist thinking of it in human terms, so she thought of it as Bully, which was apt.

If she had food, she would hold up her fingertips with the food dangling in them; the grouper would charge and she would drop the food into its mouth. It had no desire to bite her fingers, but it was a clumsy eater, consuming anything in its path, and though its teeth were small its jaws were extremely powerful, and a minor slip could result in crushed or shredded fingertips.

Today she had nothing for the grouper, so she held up a closed fist. The animal seemed to understand the gesture, for it made a halfhearted grab for her fist, then turned, flapped its tail in her face and moved off a few yards, there to hover in case she should, after all, produce something edible.

A shadow above crossed one of the chutes of yellow light, and Paloma looked up. One behind another, a procession of hammerhead sharks passed overhead in parade. Their silver-gray bodies were as sleek as bullets, and the sunlight touched the ripples of moving muscle and made them sparkle.

Paloma loved the hammerheads, for they seemed somehow to focus her inchoate thoughts about God and

nature. They were a weird and implausible-looking
animal—sinuous sledgehammers, with an eye on each
end of the hammer's head and a mouthful of teeth
beneath—and since once in a great while they had
attacked a human and otherwise accomplished absolutely nothing good for man or beast, they must
definitely be bad: That, at least, was how Viejo had
rated them as living creatures.

And yet, if ever there was an animal that seemed
to Paloma peculiarly blessed, it was the hammerhead.
Sharks had for so long been so critical to the island's
survival that over the generations facts about them—
salted here and there with myths—had been assimilated
by most islanders. It was common knowledge, for example, that hammerheads like these had survived, un-
changed, for about thirty million years. Except when
they were injured or ill, they had no enemies on earth,
save man. They had ample food, complete freedom,
and sufficient company and kin for whatever their needs
might be.

It was Jobim, however, who had given Paloma perspective to add to the facts, who had shown her how
perfectly the hammerheads were suited to their lives.
They were simple and speedy and efficient, and, he
reminded her, unlike man they made neither waste nor
war.

So to Paloma, the hammerheads were perfect, and
she saw nothing in them but beauty. She wished Viejo
could see them from down here, from where they lived
in nature. From where he saw them—writhing in agony
in a boat or clubbed to death and stinking on a broiling
beach—they could only appear grotesque.

Paloma pushed off the rock and swam down a few
more feet, into a thin valley between two big boulders.
There, in the sand, a triggerfish was darting back and

forth, frantic, its tail quivering, its gill flaps fluttering. At first, Paloma thought the triggerfish was wounded, for its movements were erratic and it was encircled by three, then five, then nine or ten other fish, all of which seemed determined to attack it.

A Scotch parrot fish—with tartanlike scales and beaked mouth—charged the smaller triggerfish, which parried with a flurry of twisting bites. The parrot fish retreated.

Immediately an angelfish dashed forward, feinted at the triggerfish, then banked and tried to get at the sand beneath the triggerfish, but it, too, was driven off.

Now Paloma realized what was happening. The triggerfish's egg deposit had been discovered by the other fish in the little valley, and they were ganging up on the triggerfish, trying to divert it long enough for one or another of them to dash in and root out and eat the cache of eggs.

Paloma felt instinctively parental toward the eggs, and so she swam into the midst of the flurry and flashed her hands around; the invaders dispersed. But the triggerfish's natural assumption was that Paloma was another thief, albeit a larger one, and its response was to bite her earlobe.

Paloma moved away, smiling inside but sad because she knew that before long the triggerfish would lose out to the odds. Once an egg deposit was discovered, it was as good as gone. Still, she told herself, that was the way it was supposed to be, an example of nature in balance. If all the eggs of every triggerfish hatched, and all the hatchlings grew to maturity, the sea would be choked with triggerfish.

Now she began to feel the telltale ache in her lungs, the hollow sensation that she imagined as the lungs themselves searching for more bits of air to consume.

Her temples began to pound, not painfully but noisily. She pushed off the bottom and kicked easily toward the surface, trailing a stream of bubbles behind.

Her rule was to rest for five or ten minutes between dives, for then she could dive again and again without pain or fatigue. If she did not rest, she found that each successive dive would have to be shorter and the ache in her lungs would be sharper.

So she hung on the anchor line and drew deep breaths of the warm, moist air and occasionally looked underwater through her mask to see if anything new or special had arrived in the neighborhood of the seamount.

Perhaps today she would see a golden *cabrío*, the rare, solitary grouper of a yellow so rich and unblemished that when it hung motionless in the water it appeared to be cast of solid gold. Or perhaps there would be a pulsing cloud of barracudas, whose silver backs caught the sunlight and were transformed into a shower of needles.

Once she had even seen a whale shark, but that was an encounter no reasonable person could hope to have again.

Her first reaction had been shock, and then, for a fragment of a second, terror, and then, when she realized exactly what it was, a shiver and tingle and flood of warmth through her stomach.

The whale shark had risen from the bottom, gliding so slowly that it seemed almost to be floating, an animal so huge that in the cloudy water Paloma could not see its head and tail at the same time. But she could determine its color—a speckled, mustardy yellow—and that told her there was no danger. The whale shark ate plankton and tiny shrimps and other minute life.

Jobim had cautioned her that she might see a whale

shark out here, had tried to prepare her for the shock she would feel at her first sight of the leviathan.

"There is one way he can hurt you," Jobim had said without a hint of jest.

"Tell me." Paloma imagined stinging spines or molarlike teeth that could crush her bones.

"If you see his mouth open, and you swim to it and you pry open his jaws and you squeeze yourself inside and force the jaws closed behind you."

"Papa!"

"Even then, I don't think he'd like you very much. He'd shake his head and spit you out."

Paloma had jumped on her father and wrapped her arms and legs around him and tried to bite his neck.

When she had positively identified the whale shark, she had swum down to meet this largest of all fish, and just then it had slowed its ambling pace enough so that she could touch the head and run her hand down the endless ridges of the back. It did not show any signs of acknowledging her presence, but continued its lazy cruise, propelled by gentle sweeps of its tail. And when finally Paloma's hand reached the tail, she had hiccoughed in awe, for the tail fin alone was as tall as she was. And as it moved back and forth, it pushed before it a wave of water so powerful that it cast her away in a helpless tumble.

The whale shark had then moved off into the gray-green gloom, relentlessly, seeming almost dutiful—as if programmed to follow a course, or a pattern of courses, set by nature countless millions of years ago.

But today, as Paloma lay on the surface of the sea, with her face in the water, breathing through a rubber tube—wanting to be part of the sea but confined to the world of air—she saw below a scene of routine and undisturbed daily life. It was a life of ceaseless movement, constant vigilance, perpetual caution, and perfect harmony.

A change of pressure told her something was happening, or was about to happen—a slight alteration in the way the water felt around her body. It felt tighter, seemed to press on her, as if something of great mass and size was moving toward her at high speed.

Reflexively, she back-pedaled in the water, trying to get away from this thing, whatever it was, that she could feel but couldn't see, that felt as if it was coming closer and closer, for the pressure on her body was beginning to lift her out of the water.

Then she saw it, a black thing.

It was larger than she was, larger even than her boat. It was soaring up at her. It was winged, and the wings swept up and down with such power that everything before and beside them was tossed aside, scattered. She could see a mouth that was a black cavern, and it was flanked by two horns, and the horns were aimed at Paloma, as if to grip her and stuff her into the gaping hole.

It was a manta ray. And even though she knew, rationally, that she had nothing to fear, she felt a rush of panic. Why was it coming straight at her? Why didn't it turn?

Her body was rising higher in the water, driven by the pressure wave forced before the manta. Her breath caught in her throat. Sparks shot through her brain, impelling an action, contradicting the impulse, impelling another action, contradicting that. She was paralyzed.

When it was no more than a few feet from Paloma, the manta tilted its wing and arched its back, changing its angle to display a belly of sheer and shiny white. Five trembling gills were on either side, crescent wings like slices of the winter moon.

The ray rushed up through the water and broke the surface, a perfect triangle of solid flesh that should not be able to fly but was flying, as it broke free of the sea and reached for the sky.

In Paloma's head, sight and feeling gave way to sound, for there was a thick and deafening roar, an enveloping, infernal boom, like the sound the wind makes at the height of a hurricane.

Paloma's head rose with the manta, and her eyes followed it as it flew high in the air, shedding diamonds of water. At the top of its arc it hung for a fraction of a second, a titan of shimmering black against the sun that rimmed it with a halo of gold.

Then it fell backward, showing its belly; it smashed flat against the pewter sea. The water erupted, and the sound seemed to carry the same reckless violence as a thunderclap that cracks the clouds close by.

Now Paloma could let out her breath, a whoosh of excitement. She had seen mantas jump before—young ones especially, at twilight usually—but always from a distance. They seemed to be flipping in happy somersaults.

But mantas couldn't be "happy." This was what the islanders called an "old" animal, and by "old" they meant low and primitive and stupid. Its cousins were the sharks and the skates and the other rays. The wisdom was that "old" animals could not know pleasure or pain, happiness or distress. Their brains were efficient but small, their capacities limited.

And Paloma agreed with most of this wisdom, for Jobim had taught her that it was wrong ever to think of animals in human terms. It deprived animals of what was most precious about them—their individuality, their place in nature. Jobim had special contempt for people who tried to tame wild animals, to make them pets, to train them to do what he called "people tricks."

It was, he had supposed, a way for people to be less afraid of an animal, for an animal that could be taught to, say, walk on its hind legs or beg for food seemed less wild, less threatening, more human. But it also made the animal seem less whole.

But what, then, was this manta doing? Why had it jumped right beside her, when the sea was empty for miles around? The island wisdom said that mantas jumped out of water only to rid themselves of parasites—small animals that attached themselves to a larger animal and fed on it. Some of these parasites were burrowers, little crabs or snails or worms, that dug holes in the manta and fed on its flesh. Then there were fish called remoras, which had sucker discs on top of their heads by which they fastened themselves to the host animal. They were not parasites but, rather, hitchhikers, for they did no harm to the manta and fed only on scraps of food the manta missed.

According to Jobim, by leaping into the air the manta deprived the parasites of oxygen (for, like fish, the parasites got their oxygen from water, not air), and the sudden shock caused the parasite to let go. If the shock alone did not dislodge the parasites, then being slammed down on the water would surely knock them loose.

Paloma saw the logic in what Jobim had said. But on this manta she had seen no parasites, and in its jumps there was a sense of vigor, of energy, of excitement.

The island wisdom about manta rays had always encouraged Paloma to fear them. Careless sailors and fishermen were said to have been consumed by mantas.

Disobedient children were threatened with being cast adrift amid a school of mantas.

And then, Paloma remembered, one day a few months ago she had been diving on the seamount and had seen a manta from the surface. It had been flying through the water with the grace of a hawk, rising and falling on its wind of water. Paloma recalled now how surprised she had been that none of the other creatures on the seamount had acted afraid of the manta. They had not scurried out of its way, had not dashed for cover in the rocks. They had seemed to know that the manta would avoid them—gently lifting a wing to pass over a pair of groupers or dipping it to pass beneath a school of jacks.

On the edge of the seamount that day, beyond a small school of fish, the water had been gray and turbid, signaling the presence of a cloud of plankton swept up into shallow water. The manta had headed for the plankton, and as it approached the cloud, it had surprised Paloma again: Its dreadful horns unfurled and showed themselves for what they actually were—floppy fins. The manta had spread the fins and used them like arms, sweeping the plankton-rich water into its mouth.

The manta had made three passes through the cloud of plankton and then, evidently satisfied, had flown up and away.

Now, holding onto her pirogue, feeling her pulse slow and her breathing become more regular, Paloma waited, her head out of water, to see if today's manta would jump once more. She wanted to see it as it broke the surface, to hear the roar and experience the explosion again.

When, after a few moments, the manta did not reappear, she put her face in the water and turned in a circle.

But the manta must have gone off into the deep, for life on the seamount had resumed its routine. Paloma decided to dive back down to the bottom.

She took deep breaths and sped down the anchor line. Finding the same rock on the bottom, she locked her legs around it. She half expected things to be different here on the bottom, as if the drama on the surface should have provoked changes below. But all was the same: The same fish patrolled the same rocks, the same eels poked their heads out of the same holes, the same jacks sped by in search of food.

There had been one change which, inevitable though it was, made her feel wistful nonetheless. Nearby, in the little valley, the triggerfish was still darting back and forth. But now the fish was alone. Nothing was taunting it, nothing attacking. And its motion was different from what it had been, less aggressive yet more desperate. Such, at least, was Paloma's interpretation, for she knew that the triggerfish's eggs had finally been taken and that the fish was searching for them in hopeless frenzy.

Another fish swam slowly before Paloma's mask. It was a fat thing, with tiny fins that seemed far too small for its body. She waited until the fish was only a few inches away, then lashed out with both hands and grabbed it around the body. She held it very lightly, anticipating what would happen.

The fish struggled for a second and then, like a balloon, began to inflate. The scales on its back stood on end and became stiff white thorns. Its lips pursed and its eyes receded into the swelling body and its fins, which now looked absurdly small, flapped in fury.

Paloma juggled this spiny football on her fingers for a moment, then held its bulbous face to hers. The pufferfish could not struggle long. It had done all it could—

become a thoroughly unappetizing meal—so now it simply stared back at Paloma. Gently, she released it in open water, and it fluttered quickly away. As it neared the shelter of the rocks, gradually it deflated. The thorns on its back lay down and once again became scales. By the time it reached a familiar crevice, it was slim enough to squirt through to safety.

Paloma began to hear anew the distant throbbing in her temples. It was still faint, not urgent; she had plenty of time to get to the surface. But by nature and Jobim's training, she was cautious—better to have more than enough air left when she reached the surface than not enough when she was still far below. And so she kicked off the bottom and rose, facing the hill of rocks and coral.

Ten feet above the bottom, she saw an oyster growing on the underside of a boulder. She reached behind her and slid her knife from her belt and, with a single twist of her wrist, cut the oyster away.

The throbbing in her head was louder now, urging her to hurry up to where she belonged. Often she wished she had gills like a fish and could breathe water. But at times like this, she wanted only one thing: air. She kicked hard, and her strong legs drove her upward with a speed that plastered her hair over the faceplate of her mask.

She popped through the surface, spat, and gulped a breath of air, then clung to the side of the pirogue and drew more breaths until her body was fully nourished with oxygen. Then she dropped the oyster into the pirogue, pulled herself aboard, and lay on the bottom, facing the sun and its warmth.

When she was warm and dry, she used her knife to split the mango and dig out the sweet, juicy fruit. She tossed the mango rind overboard and watched, fascinated, as it was savaged by a school of tiny, yellow-and-black-striped fish.

These sergeant-major fish were everywhere, on reefs and rocks, in deep water and shallow. They appeared suddenly, from nowhere, at the slightest trace of food of any kind. They ate fruit, bones, nuts, bread, meat, vegetables, feces, paper and—now and then—they nibbled on Paloma's toes.

They were daring and fearless and voracious and fast, and the nicest thing Paloma could say about them was that they were so small. A mutant sergeant major, a specimen of, say, a hundred pounds, would be a genuine horror.

She let her imagination roam further, envisioning a sergeant major the size of a whale shark, and found herself once again admiring the precision of the balance nature had maintained, over thousands of years, among all its living things.

She picked up the scraggly oyster and held it in one hand. With the other hand, she guided the point of her knife to the rough slit between the two halves of the shell. Oysters weren't like clams, which you could open cleanly and easily, with a cut and a twist and a scoop. Oysters were ragged and sharp and coated with slimy growths, and if you weren't very careful you'd stab yourself in the palm of your hand. And the cut would bleed, so you couldn't dive anymore that day, and it would probably get infected so you couldn't go into the water for several days, and it might get so badly infected that you would fall sick and have to go to bed or even on the boat to La Paz to see the doctor.

The point was, best to be careful opening oysters.

Patiently, she pried around the edges of the shell until she found a place where the knife could probe inside.

She felt the knife point touch the muscle that held the shell together; slowly she sawed there.

Most people on the island would not eat oysters. They were thought to be unsafe. Some people who had eaten them became violently sick to their stomachs, and over the years a few had died.

The truth was that the only bad oyster was an oyster left too long in the sun. They died soon and spoiled instantly, and a spoiled oyster was a ticket to the hospital in La Paz.

But an oyster fresh from the sea was a delicacy, something cool and rich and salty and pure. Paloma cut through the last bit of muscle and prised open the shell and saw then that this oyster was the greatest delicacy of all.

Inside, nestled in the shimmering gray meat, was the prize. It was misshapen and wrinkled, its color mottled, and it was only half the size of Paloma's little fingernail. But it was a pearl.

IV

PALOMA PLUCKED THE pearl from its shell and let it roll
around in the palm of her hand.

Now she had twenty-seven.

It had taken her more than a year to find the others,
but her progress had been steady: roughly, an average
of two a month. It had been more than six weeks,
however, since she had found the last one, and she had
begun to wonder. Was it possible that on the whole seamount there were only twenty-six pearl-bearing oysters?
She needed at least forty pearls, preferably fifty.

Finding number twenty-seven renewed her hope. She
closed her fist around the little pearl and looked at the
sky and said, "Thank you."

Her thanks were directed, in a vague but concentrated
way, at her father. He was dead, she knew that, but she
could not accept the premise that dead meant finished
forever. She was lonely for, and needed, her father, and
so in her mind she fashioned a presence for him. She did

not think of him as alive, exactly, but simply as existing somewhere, still available for her to talk to and ask for help and share private things with. For in all her life he had been the only person she had felt comfortable sharing things with.

The fact that her father was out there somewhere (and it was a fact for her; she felt it strongly) was an enormous help to her. She didn't hear his voice, but he comforted her nevertheless. A sympathetic presence who listened with patience to her problems, he never agreed or disagreed, never criticized or praised. And somehow, being able to explore events and alternatives this way seemed to guide Paloma, help her toward a direction and a solution.

Of course, sometimes she felt foolish, and was glad no one saw her as she seemed to be talking to the sky or the wind or an empty room. But there *was* something there. Whether it was she who willed it there, projected it there, didn't matter; it was there, whatever "it" was. She avoided precise definition, preferring to leave it as a concept amorphous enough so as not to be confining, a spirit, accessible, clear. And while surely she needed her father, she also felt that he needed her, and that they were working as a team.

Shortly before he died, Jobim had recruited Paloma into a conspiracy.

Only a few months from now, Jobim and Miranda would have marked twenty years of marriage. He had wanted to give his wife something special. Since he had no money beyond that which fed and clothed them, he could not buy her something fine. So he had decided he would have to make the gift himself. And whatever he determined to make would have to be made in secret —he could not hope to deceive Miranda as he had deceived Paloma about the pirogue. And if it must be a secret, it must be small enough to conceal.

Yet it could not be a wood carving or a clay figure or a decoration fashioned of seashells. Anyone could carve wood or collect seashells. It had to be something that only he could do, so that for Miranda it would be a gift direct from his heart to hers.

Once he had found the answer, it seemed obvious: pearls, a necklace of natural pearls. Of all the islanders, only he (and, through his teaching, Paloma) pursued the ancient skills of diving for and identifying and collecting and opening pearl oysters. He had maintained the skills only for his own amusement, for pearling was no longer profitable. The pearl beds had been depleted more than a generation ago, but even if they were to come back, the market for natural pearls had all but disappeared. People now preferred cultured pearls; they were rounder, had more luster.

Jobim did not like cultured pearls. "They are prettier, and they do come from the sea, and they make a nice necklace," he told Paloma. "But they are not natural. They are man trying to improve on nature. Nature is one miracle after another. Man can't improve it; he can only change it."

Jobim had found only five pearls before he died, but he had helped Paloma refine her pearling skills. And so she had taken upon herself the task of completing the necklace. She and Jobim had begun something; he had gone away before being able to complete it; she would complete it for him.

She thought often of how she would give the necklace to her mother. She didn't want to seem overly sentimental, but, on the other hand, she wanted to be sure that Miranda knew the necklace was a gift from Jobim, no matter who had gathered most of the pearls.

One of Jobim's earliest lessons to his children was that truth was almost always preferable to lies. It was not only a moral conclusion; truth was usually easier. For one thing, it was easier to remember. But here truth was impossible, so Paloma had decided to weave the simplest lie she could. She would tell her mother that Jobim had collected the pearls and had hidden them with the intention of stringing them just before the anniversary date.

"Thank heavens," Paloma would say. "One day he swore me to secrecy and told me where they were, in case something should happen to him."

There would be happiness and sorrow and nostalgia and tears. The important thing for Paloma was that all the emotion would be directed not at her but at her father—at his memory or his spirit or whatever image Miranda still held of him.

Paloma tucked the pearl into a narrow crack in the wood on one side of the pirogue, so it couldn't roll around or spill out if the pirogue should tip. Then she lay back to rest for a few minutes, for she had found that to dive too soon after eating was to invite a painful knot in her side or, sometimes, to bring up bile in her throat, which could be very dangerous and was inevitably very frightening. If bile was rising, vomit would follow soon behind, and there was nothing worse than to vomit underwater. The gag reflex would force a spasmodic intake of breath, which would bring salt water into her lungs, which would force a violent cough and another breath and would drown her.

She fell asleep. When she awoke no more than half an hour later, she recalled vividly that she had dreamed of a gull flying round and round her pirogue and laughing at her.

It was a recollection more curious than uncomfortable, for she associated nothing whatever with any of her dreams—except those about her father, which were sometimes disturbing when she couldn't separate dream conversations from genuine ones.

Paloma slipped overboard and cleaned her mask. She grabbed the anchor line and took deep breaths and pulled for the bottom. Ten feet from the surface she stopped.

Something was wrong. The seamount had changed. She was disoriented. Was it her eyes? Had more time passed than she realized? Nothing looked the same. An entire section of the seamount seemed covered in black.

She closed her eyes and willed herself to stay calm, to sort through conflicting images. When she felt more composed, she opened her eyes and looked down again. And then she could see what had perplexed her. Not five feet away was the largest manta ray she had ever seen.

It was like a black cloak, or a big blanket that, from this short distance, blocked out most of her view of the seamount.

It was not only the proximity of the giant that had deceived her; it was also the fact that the animal was not moving at all. It was lying absolutely still in the water, as if suspended from an invisible ceiling. It did not look alive.

But it had to be alive, for how else would it have gotten there? Dead, it would have sunk to the bottom.

She dropped farther down, expecting the animal at any moment to shrug its wing and move away. But the manta continued to hover, motionless.

Her toes were within inches of the manta's back, and now she could see nothing of the seamount below. It was like landing on a black field that extended almost as far as she could see. The ray had to be more than twenty feet across, for she judged that she could have lain down four times across its wings and still not covered them tip to tip.

This is the grandfather of all mantas, she thought. Why is it drifting around? Is it dying?

Paloma had to go up for air. Making as little stir as possible in the water, she floated up. As the distance between her and the manta grew, she gained perspective on the whole animal, and she could see that there was a reason it was not behaving normally. Long, thin things were trailing beneath and behind it.

Her face broke water. She breathed in and out several times, each breath a bit deeper than the last, drew one final breath that seemed to suck air down into her feet, and went down again.

The manta had not moved. This time she approached it from the front, and immediately she saw what was wrong.

Behind the "horn" on the left side, the animal's flesh was torn in a broad, deep gash. Knotted ropes were embedded in the shredded flesh, their ends dangling loose, like tails.

The manta must have become fouled in a fisherman's net, then panicked, and flailing frantically to get free, driven its great bulk against the taut ropes, forcing them to bite even deeper into its flesh. Finally, it had escaped —undoubtedly, Paloma thought, leaving an angry fisherman to curse his wretched fate and declare that all mantas were devilfish that deserved to die.

But the manta's victory was illusory, for it was bound to die. Paloma had seen many wounded animals—cut or hooked or scraped or bitten—and she knew that in the sea there was no time of truce, there was no mercy.

The wound had weakened the manta, and because the ropes still festered in the open sore there had been no chance for healing to begin. Unable to pursue its food, the manta could not eat as much as it should. The less it ate, the weaker it would become; the weaker it became, the less it could eat.

Before long, the manta would begin to emit the silent signals of distress that would be received and interpreted by every animal on the seamount—especially by the larger animals, the predators.

First would come the tiny, voracious fish, like the sergeant majors. The signals they interpreted would tell them that it was safe to ravage the bits of dying flesh in the open wound. They would swim on the wound, opening it further.

The manta would grow weaker still. Little by little, it would appear to be, and would become, less and less formidable. Its sensory transmitters, incapable of human guile, would continue to broadcast signals of increasing vulnerability. Inevitably, the manta would be committing inadvertent suicide.

Sharks would begin to gather, circling at a distance, their receivers assessing each new signal, until one of them—particularly hungry, perhaps, or agitated or perhaps simply bold—would break the circle and dart in at the manta and tear away a ragged bite of meat.

The end would come quickly then, in an explosion of blood and a cloud of shreds of skin and sinew.

Paloma could hear the pulse in her temples as she swam down toward the manta. The animal knew she was there—the eye beneath the gaping wound followed her as she drew near—but it did not move.

Her momentum was carrying her past the manta, over its head. She put out a hand to stop herself, and her fingers curled around a hard ledge above the mouth and between the two horns. The flesh there felt firm—like a taut muscle—but slick, for it was coated with a natural mucous slime. The feeling didn't startle Paloma, for she had touched many fish and had felt the same slime. It was a shield against bacteria and other things in the rich salt water that would cause illness or injury.

Jobim had taught her that if a fish you didn't need was caught in your net, and if you picked it up, intending to release it, you had to be careful that your fingers didn't scrape away the protective coating from the fish's skin. If the slime was removed, a sore might develop on that spot, or a burrowing creature might discover the opening and settle in and begin to gnaw away. A fish that had been handled too much before being released usually didn't survive for long.

Apparently, the manta was no more startled by her touch than was Paloma. It did not bolt from her; it did not twitch or shudder or shake. It didn't move. It just lay there, floating, suspended in midwater.

It has no fear of me, Paloma thought. And why should it? It knows no enemies. But I am a strange animal and I am touching this manta, and it is not a common occurrence in nature for one wild animal to allow another to touch like this. Still, mantas do put up with remoras stuck onto their bodies and dragging behind. Maybe, as far as this manta knows, I'm just a big remora.

A swift flow of water was holding Paloma horizontal, her flippers fluttering like a flag in a high wind. Somehow, the manta was managing to stay perfectly still in the strong current, without seeming to exert any effort at all. If Paloma were to let go, she would be swept away.

Now she reached with her other hand for the same ledge of muscle, and she tucked her knees up underneath her and knelt on the manta's back. The skin was like a shark's, not really skin but a carpet made up of millions of tiny toothlike things. They all faced to the rear, and so as Paloma's hand stroked the skin from front to back, it felt as smooth as a greased ceramic bowl. But as her knees inched up, back to front, the manta's skin, like coarse sandpaper, abraded them.

The terrible gash in the manta's flesh was beside Paloma's left hand. Some of the knotted ropes were buried several inches deep. Most of the flesh was whitish-gray, but some was pink and some yellow.

Once, the year before Jobim had died, a strange organism had drifted over the seamount and attacked the schooling jacks, causing suppurating sores on their sides. Jobim had caught one of the jacks and shown it to Paloma, pointing out the different flesh tones of the ailing fish: White-gray was healthy, pink was inflamed, and yellow signaled the generation of a puslike substance that showed that the animal's body had activated its defense mechanisms.

A few of the ropes snaked out of the manta's wound and trailed behind, tugged by the rushing water. Does it feel pain? Paloma wondered. It must. That's probably why it stays so still: Movement would tug the ropes harder and make them shift and wiggle, and that would hurt more.

Gripping the ledge tightly with her right hand, she let go with her left and reached for the rope snarled nearest to the surface of the wound. It was a jumble of knots and kinks, and it vibrated as the water flowed through it.

Be quick, Paloma told herself, like when the doctor gives an injection. Grab it, pull it free and cast it away, all before the manta knows what's happening.

She threaded her fingers deep into the mess of rope and made a fist around as much as her hand could grasp. Then she yanked.

It was as if she had thrown a switch that turned the manta on. The animal heaved both wings at once, churning up a maelstrom that threw Paloma off its back and tumbled her into a spinning somersault.

By the time she had righted herself and cleared her mask and waited for the storm of bubbles to dissipate, the manta was flying away into the dark water, ropes fluttering behind. It did not make a sound, but Paloma imagined that she heard an outraged wail of pain.

She kicked toward the surface, trailing some of the ropes in her hand, wishing she had had time to grab more, hoping that by removing some of them she might have increased the manta's chances of survival.

V

THE SUN WAS still high when Paloma left the seamount and started to paddle toward home. She was tired and hungry and cold. But most of all, she was lonely.

It was a curious contradiction that the better her day on the seamount was, the lonelier she felt when it was over, and because today had been particularly exciting, she felt acutely lonely.

The problem was not that her experiences were solitary—she liked being alone—but that there was no one on the island with whom she could share the wonder, the exhilaration, of her day when she got home. There was no friend who would understand, no sister or cousin who would care. In fact, there was no one on the island to whom she had confided the existence of her seamount or what she did all day in her boat.

There were no other girls Paloma's age on the island. Why, no one knew: a quirk of nature. There were plenty of females many years older—women now, with children of their own—and plenty of boys. But no girls. From the moment Paloma had been old enough to know what it was to be alone, she had been alone. Of course, she had her mother, but there were limits to what she felt comfortable talking to her mother about, and there were limits to what Miranda wanted to hear.

Paloma paddled harder, trying to stroke away the loneliness, to erase it with sheer muscle power. And she was trying, as well, to warm up, for gooseflesh had risen on her arms and legs, and the fine yellow hairs were standing on end.

The water never felt cold to her—and it *was* warm, at least eighty-five degrees—but no matter how warm it felt, it was always cooler than Paloma's body temperature, so spending hours in it sucked the heat from her body and caused its temperature to drop. It was not a dangerous cold—"You can live for a week in this water," Jobim had told her, adding with a grin, "if the sun doesn't cook you or something doesn't eat you." But it was uncomfortable.

She could have combated the cold, however, and eased her hunger, too, by gaining weight. A layer of fat made a fine insulator. But she was reluctant to gain weight, to grow fat, any sooner than necessary. Being fat would slow her down, take away her agility and worst of all, signal that she was just like all the other women of Santa Maria Island.

For them, fatness seemed to be a natural progression in life. As girls they were slender; in their late teens or early twenties they became robust; in their mid-to-late twenties they were stocky, in their thirties fat and in their forties mountainous. (Paloma's mother was about to turn forty, and over the past few years her figure had gradually disappeared, its contours absorbed into her trunk.) Those who survived into their sixties or seventies often shrank back to whippet thinness.

Paloma saw herself as different. She hoped, prayed, *knew* that she was special. At least she had been special to her father.

It had been Jobim who made her feel special, had in effect decreed that she be special. After the second of Jo's accidents underwater, the one that finally convinced Jobim that his son would never be at home in the sea and would instead have to spend his life upon it, after Jobim had begun to tutor Paloma and had discovered how naturally and quickly she took to the sea and had determined that she would become a person *of* the sea, he had told Miranda that their daughter was not to be compelled to follow the normal path to womanhood, was not to be confined to the house and the pots and the washboard. He would take her with him and would teach her things about the sea and would teach her how to learn other things on her own. She would of course contribute to the household eventually, but how and what she would contribute must be left up to her.

Miranda had tried to argue, but Jobim was a man who, when he had made up his mind about something important, tended to reinforce his decision to himself until he became impossible to argue with. And Miranda knew that it was important—even vital—to Jobim that one of his children follow him into the sea.

What Jobim did not know, and what Miranda could not bring herself to tell him, was that by taking Paloma to sea he was taking her forever away from her mother, depriving Miranda of the solace that a daughter was supposed to supply to a woman. He was condemning Miranda to a daily loneliness that would sadden her for the rest of her life, for by the time of Jobim's death,

Paloma's independence had been so firmly established that Miranda could not have changed it even if she had tried. Not only did Paloma relish her way of life, but now she felt an obligation to her father to live as he had guided her to. She saw her life as having no limits. Perhaps the limits were there, and if so, someday she would confront them. But not yet.

Paloma recognized, however, that she had responsibilities to her mother, one of which contributed to her decision to return home in the middle of the afternoon. It was important that the people in her mother's world not think that Paloma considered herself too good for everyday chores.

"It is one thing to be quiet and alone and even a bit strange," Viejo had said to her one day. "People will call that growing pains and let it pass. But you must not remove yourself altogether. People will not understand. They will resent you and dislike you, become your enemies, and you do not want any more enemies than necessary."

Paloma did not want any enemies at all. And so, every few days she returned home in time to be with her mother and help her hang out the wash or prepare the meal or clean the house. Almost as important as doing these daughter things was to be seen doing them, for then the other women would cluck and mutter that Paloma was a good girl, after all, that she was sensitive to her mother's great loss, that she might turn out to be a source of comfort in her mother's old age. And so on.

It was a gesture; Paloma knew it and Miranda knew it. Miranda didn't need help; she felt she didn't have enough to do as it was. But neither did she need the patronizing sympathy of others. Miranda was grateful for the gesture, and for Paloma's presence.

When Paloma reached the dock, Miranda and the

other women were washing clothes. Beside the dock was a shelf of flat rocks that led into the water. The women gathered there and soaked their clothes and pounded soap into them with stones and rinsed them. They piled the clean clothes into baskets that would be taken up the hill for a final, fresh-water rinsing.

Paloma knelt beside Miranda and pounded clothes. No one acknowledged her arrival; the women chattered on around her. They were not ignoring her: To the contrary, they were accepting her—quietly, naturally, as if she had been there all along. It was their gesture to Miranda, for to have greeted Paloma and asked her questions would have directed attention to what was politely regarded as Paloma's peculiarity. No other girl went out on the sea all day long and did God-knows-what.

Sometimes Paloma felt like a person with a chronic affliction, like a spastic tic. People's attitude seemed to be: Poor thing, she can't help it, let's just ignore it. It increased her sense of being alone. But in another way she was glad for the treatment, for it reinforced her feeling of being special.

Paloma never volunteered information about what she had seen and done during the day. Most of the women would not have believed her, and that would have embarrassed Miranda. Those that did believe her would not want to hear what she had to say, for it went against all they had been taught about the sea.

From birth, most of the children of the islands were told that the sea was hostile. The people lived from the sea, could not possibly have existed without it, and yet it was viewed not as an ally but as an adversary. The attitude made no sense to Paloma, for she had been taught exactly the opposite, and once she had asked Viejo where the hostility had come from. "It has always been," he said with a shrug. "The sea does not give; man takes from it. Perhaps it began as a way to make man feel stronger, that he has dominion over the sea as well as over the animals."

"I think it's silly," Paloma had said.

"It may be," Viejo had nodded. "But it is the way things are."

To the women who washed and cooked and cleaned and never went on the water, the sea was alien and dangerous, populated by creatures that were ferocious, slimy, poisonous, starved for human flesh. They were comfortable with that view of the sea, and they would not have welcomed contradictions from a young girl.

As excited as Paloma was when she returned to the dock, as tempted to tell everyone what wonders she had encountered today, she restrained herself. She would wait to tell her mother when they were alone.

When the washing was done, Paloma picked up the heavy basket of wet clothes and followed Miranda up the hill. With a hand pump they washed the salt off the clothes, then draped them over a line behind the house.

They worked in silence, but it was a busy silence, for Paloma wanted very much to tell her mother about the manta ray and Miranda knew Paloma had something she wanted to say, and that she was trying to find a way to tell her.

Paloma did not want to frighten Miranda, so she could not say how big the manta was, nor how close to it she had gotten—let alone that she had knelt on its back and been tossed off violently. And she had to reassure Miranda that no one else knew what she had been doing, that no one else would know, that it would not become a subject of public gossip. What Paloma did all day every day caused enough chatter; fooling around with a giant devilfish might get her branded as a witch.

Miranda had had a husband whose reputation was as a rebel and a troublemaker. She had a son who spent all his time concocting harebrained schemes to make money—enough money to get him off the island and into a technical school in Mexico City, where the Lord alone knew what would happen to him. To add to those two a daughter who was a witch would be altogether too much for her to bear.

By now, the sun had dropped low and had begun to turn red. A light breeze was blowing through the hanging clothes, and the tails of the shirts made soft snapping sounds. Miranda sniffed and nodded and was satisfied; it was a good breeze.

There were three regular breezes that blew over Santa Maria Island. One was bad for drying clothes, one was fair, and one was good. The east wind was bad, because it blew across the dry, dusty eastern part of the island and carried dirt and dust with it. Clothes that had dried in an east wind felt gritty and itchy. Breezes from the west and south were fair. They came over the water. On dry days they carried a faint smell of the sea, but on humid days they were heavy with mist and salt. Clothes took forever to dry, and felt clammy.

This was a breeze from the north. It was dry and fresh and sweet because it had traveled over the highest part of the island, where cacti and wild desert flowers grew. It was a small thing, but Miranda's life was made of small things, good and bad, and because the breeze was good she was pleased.

They walked inside the house and began to prepare the fire for the evening meal.

"I saw a giant manta ray today," Paloma said at last.

"That's nice," said Miranda, without looking up from the fireplace where she was smoothing out the dead ashes before laying new wood.

"It was wounded. I think it got fouled in a fisherman's nets."

Miranda started to say "That's nice" again, but it seemed inappropriate, so all she said was, "Oh?"

"It didn't move well. There were ropes hanging out of the wound. It must have been in very bad pain."

This time Miranda had nothing to say, so she nodded.

"I wanted to help it, but . . ."

"God will take care of it, He will decide." Miranda spoke fast, as if spitting the words out in a rush would add emphasis, would convince Paloma not to meddle. It was like a person in an argument he knows he is losing who decides, as a last recourse, to shout.

"Well then," Paloma said, "he seems to want to let the manta die in agony, or get eaten by sharks."

"If that is His will, so be it."

"So be it," Paloma repeated. She did not intend to argue with her mother. It was an argument that could have no winners, only losers.

"What fairy tales are you telling now?" It was Jo's voice, and it came from behind Paloma.

She spun around. Jo was slouching against the doorway, a smirk on his face.

"Nothing." Paloma could not know how much Jo had overheard, but she did not want to discuss the manta ray with him. A big, wounded animal was something Jo could visualize in only one way: price per pound.

"Giant devilfish, wounded and bleeding, cared for by nurse Paloma," Jo snickered as he came into the room. "Why do you listen to this foolishness, Mama?"

"Now, Jo . . ." Miranda said, and busied herself with the fireplace.

"Sometimes I wonder if you ever leave the dock," Jo

said to Paloma. "I think maybe you sit here all day and make up tales."

"Think what you like," Paloma said.

After a moment's pause, Jo asked, "Did you really see a big manta ray?"

"Yes."

"And it didn't attack you?"

"No!"

"It must have been really hurt. Devilfish are mean."

Paloma didn't argue. If Jo wanted to believe that, she would not disrupt his fantasy.

"How big was he?"

"Big," Paloma replied. "Bigger than this room."

Jo whistled. "*He'd* bring a fancy price."

"See, Mama?" Paloma said. "He hears about an injured animal, and right away he wants to kill it."

"Well, Paloma," her mother said, "that is how we live."

"A lot you bring into the house," Jo said. "Have you ever brought home a single fish?" He held up a finger. "One fish? Even one?"

"I . . ."

"You what? You nothing. Where *was* this manta ray?"

Paloma gestured vaguely. "Out there."

"Out where?"

"In the sea."

"I know in the sea. Where in the sea?"

"It doesn't matter. He's gone."

"How do you know?"

"Because I hurt him and he flew away."

"You hurt him how?"

Paloma did not think before she spoke. "I pulled some of the ropes out of his wound and it hurt him."

Miranda stood up. She looked stricken. "You *what*?"

Jo said, "You got that close? I don't believe it."

"Don't believe it then," Paloma said, knowing that Jo believed every word.

"You *what*?" Miranda said again.

"Don't worry, Mama," Paloma said. "There wasn't any danger."

"She's right, Mama," Jo said. "There wasn't any danger, because it didn't happen."

Miranda looked from Jo to Paloma and back again, not knowing what to believe, certain only that she had something to worry about: If Paloma had done what she said, it was right to worry about her safety; if she had not, then a mother should worry about a daughter who makes up stories.

Sensing Miranda's confusion, Paloma said again, "Don't worry, Mama. the important thing is, we're all here and we're all safe."

Because Miranda wanted to believe that, she chose to, and she turned to her work.

Jo did not mention the manta again. During supper, he spoke without bluster about the day's fishing, about what he had caught and what he had hoped to catch, about how it was nice that the price for grouper had risen but the reason it had risen was that the fish were growing scarcer. Or perhaps they had just moved to other grounds.

"Do you see groupers out where you go?" he asked Paloma.

"Some."

"More than before, or less?"

Paloma shrugged. "About the same."

"You ought to bring some home."

"I don't fish."

"I know." Jo paused. "Maybe someday I should come have a look where you are."

Paloma felt all her interior warning systems go off at once, but she forced herself to stay slouched in her chair, looking nonchalant. "Wouldn't be worth your time. There's not much there."

"What keeps you going, then?"

"I study different things." She glanced at Jo. "Things Papa wanted me to study."

Jo turned away and said, tight-lipped, "Sure."

After supper, Miranda washed the plates and cups, and Paloma swabbed the table with a wet rag. Jo sat and watched.

At the end of a long silence, Jo said, "I've decided. I'd like you to teach me to dive."

"You would?" It was the first time Jo had ever asked Paloma to teach him anything. "What do you want to dive for? You said yourself it's a waste of time."

"Yeah, well, maybe I've been wrong."

Paloma looked at her mother and said, "I think Jo is sick."

"He asks you to help him," Miranda said sternly. "That is good. Now what do *you* say?"

Paloma looked at Jo. "But you know how to dive. At least, you did once."

"Yeah, well." Jo was blushing. "That didn't work out too well."

Paloma knew the story—how Jobim had led Jo into diving step by step, first in knee-deep water, then in water up to Jo's chin, then in water just over his head, then in water where the bottom was ten or fifteen feet away.

Jo had had all the lessons, knew all the rules, had

done everything his father had asked him to do—and hated every minute of it. He had felt uncomfortable, unnatural, in the water, and he felt actually threatened by deep water. But he had never dared tell his father, for Jobim's approval was the most important thing in the world. The next most important thing was to be with Jobim, to spend his days with him, and the only way to do that was to dive. So Jo had resolved to force himself.

One day, Jobim had taken Jo into the open sea for the first time. They went to where they could not see bottom, for Jobim wanted Jo to learn to gauge the depth by the feel of the water pressure on his body and by looking up at the surface from underwater.

They went down the anchor line, and at about forty feet Jo was seized by a fit of claustrophobia. Where some people feel free in open water, Jo felt trapped. The water was pressing on every bit of his body, confining him, suffocating him. There was no land anywhere, not below, not on the sides, not above. Everything was blue and heavy and oppressive. He had to leave.

He had screamed underwater and flailed with his arms and clawed his way up the anchor line. The line caught between his snorkel and his mask. Thrashing to free himself, he twisted the rubber strap even tighter around the line.

Jobim had grabbed him, tried to subdue him, but panic made Jo even stronger than he was normally, and he kicked and punched and tore his father's mask from his face.

Jo might have drowned both of them if Jobim had not felt, blindly, for his son's throat and wrapped his hand around it and squeezed until the boy lost consciousness and could be taken swiftly to the surface.

No, recalling the story of that day, Paloma could not

imagine why Jo suddenly wanted to dive again, or why suddenly he thought he could dive without panicking. But she said, "All right. If you want."

"Good. I want to see all the things you see. Tomorrow?"

Paloma spoke quickly. "No, not tomorrow. I've got . . . too many things to do." She had nothing to do, but tomorrow was too soon. She had to have time to think about what Jo could have in mind, for she could not believe that his request meant only what it said. Too many things about it were unlike him.

"Soon, then."

"Yes. Soon."

Jo stood and yawned and said good night and walked through the front door and disappeared into the night. His room was around the corner, connected to the house but separate in that it had its own entrance from outside. That was one of the privileges a boy acquired when, at the age of fourteen, he underwent the elaborate, old-fashioned mystical ritual of becoming a man. As far as Paloma could tell, all the ritual accomplished was to give the boys privileges. It didn't make them men; it called them men.

Paloma and her mother shared a corner of the main room of the house. Neither of them had any privacy in their home at any time of the day or night.

Now Paloma thought how strange it was for Jo to have asked for her help in anything. This was a significant concession: For him to acknowledge that she—a girl—might know more about something worthwhile than he did was remarkable.

She would have to be careful with Jo, take each step cautiously and try to fit it into an overall picture.

She was surprised to find that she truly cared about

what these changes in Jo might mean, and she realized it was a reflection of her loneliness, of the quiet desperation she had felt as she paddled home from the seamount that afternoon. To get along with Jo, to establish a relationship, perhaps even to make a friend—that would be a fine thing for Paloma, who had never had a friend.

VI

THE LAST TIME the relationship between Paloma and Jo had resembled a friendship had been when Paloma was five and Jo was four: Back then, they had played together happily. But soon Jo had found a pack of boys to run with, and Paloma had found herself either taunted or excluded, and she had begun to hate being a girl.

Then Jobim had taken Jo away, and left Paloma to Miranda, to be raised in Miranda's image. The two children had less and less—and finally nothing—in common.

Then had come the break, the reversal from which Jo had not recovered, when Jobim had returned him to Miranda and had taken Paloma with him, to make her the special one.

Still, for a long time Paloma had believed that it was bad to be a girl. For a while, she had dressed like a boy, cut her hair short like a boy's, learned to laugh at jokes directed at her—as if laughing *with* the joke, saying,

"Yes, isn't it ridiculous to be a girl? Aren't I foolish? Well, I won't be a girl for long, and then we'll all have a good laugh at what I used to be."

Jobim—as a male who had never wanted to be anything else—could not have understood the depth of the anxiety and confusion Paloma was feeling. But he knew generally what was wrong, deduced that it had to come from her being the only girl of her age on the island, and guessed that her feelings about herself and her sex were jumbled, confused.

So one day Jobim had taken Paloma fishing. She was quite young then and had never before been taken to sea. In fact, she had rarely been in Jobim's boat, except for holiday excursions to visit the sea-lion rookery and a few trips to La Paz.

They were alone in the boat, and Paloma was thrilled. She did not ask why she had been excused from her household chores, or where they were going. She was to be on the sea with Papa, and that was enough. The last thing she could have imagined was that Jobim intended the journey to alter Paloma's view of herself.

The sea was oily calm, so flat that the soft swells looked like bulges in a jelly, and Paloma had been able to kneel on the forward thwart and hang out over the bow of the boat. The sharp wooden prow sliced through the water like a fine blade through flesh. She thought of the surface of the sea as the skin of a huge fish, and of the bow as a knife that was filleting it for market.

Jobim had anchored the boat in what seemed to Paloma to be the middle of the sea. Actually, the boat was directly over the seamount, but Paloma had never yet been underwater, so she had no idea that the sea bottom was a landscape of different terrains. As far as she knew, the bottom was distant and dangerous, an unknown country, like death.

Jobim had baited a big hook with half a needlefish, but he did not throw the line overboard. Instead, he handed her a face mask and snorkel and told her to put them on. Then, with his own mask propped up on his forehead, he told Paloma to jump overboard and hang onto the anchor line.

"Here?" Paloma was shocked. In the middle of the sea? "Why?"

"I want to show you something about girls," Jobim had said, and though what he said made no sense to her, she obeyed and slipped over the side.

Jobim jumped into the water and hung beside her, holding the anchor rope in the crook of an elbow so as not to drift away in the current. Slowly he fed the fishing line through his fingers, dropping the baited hook down toward the seamount.

Paloma's first sight of the seamount was breathtaking, a discovery as miraculous as if she had been given a secret glimpse of heaven, for here was a world she had not known existed. It was strange and very active and very silent and (she was surprised when she recalled it later) not at all threatening. It was almost like watching a film, for although the living that was going on down there was not far away, it was somehow separate from her world, unquestionably real but wonderfully new, enchanted.

They lay together on the surface, their faces in the water, breathing through the rubber snorkel tubes. Jobim spoke to Paloma by rotating his head a quarter turn, until his mouth was out of the water, and Paloma could hear him clearly without moving: She couldn't tell whether she was receiving the sound of his voice down her snorkel tube and through her mouth or filtered through the few inches of seawater that covered her ears. Neither way made any sense to her, but she didn't care: His words came through distinctly, though they did sound hollow and far away.

The nylon fishing line was soon invisible in the water, but the bait was unmistakable—a white morsel that dangled provocatively just above the bottom and moved, not with its own rhythm like a living thing in harmony with the current, but like a dead thing caught and held.

Small fish approached the bait and hovered around it, seeming to appraise it for delicacy and danger. Jobim had made no attempt to hide the hook, and now and then a glint of steel would flash in a ray of light. Whether the fish were not enticed by the needlefish, or were scared by the hook, Paloma could not tell, but none of them went for the bait.

Then they were gone. The small fish vanished. The bait hung unattended, swaying in the current.

"Where did they go?"

"Watch," Jobim said. "Just watch."

For a moment or two, nothing happened. What had been a bustling community was now a barren plain. Paloma half expected to hear a clap of thunder or see a bolt of lightning, for such a change had to be the result of a natural drama.

And then, from the darkness at the edge of the seamount came the sharks—hammerheads, three of them, one half again as large as the other two: silent searchers moving with a relentless arrogance that broadcast their sovereignty over the seamount. Their bizarre, T-shaped heads swung slowly from side to side, gathering signals from the sea, interpreting them and sending out signals of their own. These soundless impulses preceded them everywhere, giving fair warning of their arrival, allowing all but proper prey to depart in safety.

Jobim jigged the bait, and though Paloma heard nothing new, she could see that the sharks received the message clearly, for they swung, in formation, toward the dancing piece of meat. They circled it once, then again, and then one of the smaller sharks broke the circle and darted in at the bait. Jobim jerked the line, and the bait popped up and away from the shark's mouth.

The three sharks circled again, faster now, each in turn shaking its head with a brusque, annoyed motion. They were perplexed, because something was not as it should be: They were receiving signals that reported dead meat, but the prey was not behaving as if dead.

The second of the two smaller sharks shot forward, and once more Jobim jerked the bait away. This time he did not let it down; he pulled it up toward the surface, challenging the sharks to follow it. Only one did, the largest. The other two hung below, angrily circling nothing.

The big shark did not attack the bait. It followed patiently, with sinuous grace. As it drew near, Paloma saw that this animal, which on the bottom had looked like a good-size fish, was enormous—bigger than she, bigger than Papa, almost as big as Papa's boat.

Paloma was terrified. She trusted Papa totally, knew that she would jump off a mountain or swallow needles if he said she should, but to play games with a big man-eating shark . . .

Unable to take her eyes from the advancing shark, she flailed with her free hand, desperate to grab the gunwale of the boat and pull herself to safety.

"Stop it," Jobim said. "Lie still."

Paloma lay still, but she was sure the shark could hear her heart. Were they like dogs, could they smell fear? She held her breath, hoping to mute the timpani in her chest, but that only made her heartbeat seem louder.

The bait was six or eight feet away, and the shark a foot beyond it. Jobim kept pulling, but now the shark stopped coming. It circled instead, the black eye on the end of its fleshy white "T" watching as Jobim reeled in the bait and, with a single twist, removed the hook from it.

Paloma turned with the shark, rotating like a flower petal in a tidal eddy, panicked that she might lose sight of the circling hunter: There was something unbearable about knowing that the animal was there and not being able to see it.

A movement below caught her eye. Now the other two sharks were rising. They kept their distance from the larger one, seeming to defer to it, but they were growing bolder. And though they were definitely smaller than the other shark, relativity was the only comfort: Her father was six feet tall, and each of these sharks was at least as long as he was tall.

Jobim held the half-needlefish out to the big shark and wiggled it with his fingertips. The circling pattern grew tighter. Now the shark was missing Paloma by only three or four feet as it swept by. The head was shaking actively, the crescent mouth opening and closing in expectant cadence.

Jobim pushed the needlefish out into open water, released it, and quickly drew back his hand. The shark passed by, and the fish disappeared. There had been no snapping, no biting, no shaking of the head. The shark had simply inhaled the needlefish.

It made two more tight turns around Jobim and Paloma, then gradually loosened its pattern, like a spring unwinding. Its black eye never left them, but there was no urgency to its behavior. It was waiting.

Jobim reached inside his shorts, undid a knot and came out with a whole needlefish. Paloma had not seen him do it, but in the boat he must have stuffed a plastic bag of needlefish inside his pants—out of sight of the sharks and, because the neck of the bag was tied off, out of their range of smell.

Immediately, the shark once again swept close by and resumed its tight circling pattern.

This time, Jobim broke the needlefish in two and shook both halves and then dropped them. As they fell, trailing bits of meat and puffs of oil, Jobim tapped Paloma's arm and motioned her to watch.

The smaller sharks sensed the food and rose toward it eagerly, hungrily, their heads shaking quickly. At the same time, the large shark dropped its head and raised its pectoral fins and snapped its tail back and forth, which drove the body downward like a spear.

For a moment, it seemed that the sharks must collide. All three raced toward the pieces of fish, which continued to fall together.

Paloma saw that the small sharks were bound to win, for the needlefish was falling toward them and away from the bigger shark.

When the pieces of needlefish were no more than a foot from the mouths of each of the smaller sharks— when their victory was inevitable—both, simultaneously and inexplicably, turned away. The big shark soared down upon the pieces of fish, sucking in the first piece then turning away and making a wide circle and letting the second morsel fall—utterly casual, confident that there was no hurry, that the food would be there for the taking—then banking and descending in a dive and gobbling the last bit of food.

The smaller sharks continued downward, away from

the large one, away from the food, away from conflict. They shook their heads and hunched their backs and flailed their tails.

They're like puppies, Paloma thought. They're angry and upset and there's nothing they can do about it, so they're running around yapping and chasing their tails.

The big shark returned and began once again to circle. Jobim motioned to Paloma to climb back into the boat. She didn't hesitate. Keeping her eye on the shark, she reached up and gripped the gunwale and pulled herself to the side of the boat. She took a deep breath and tested the firmness of her grasp on the wood. When Jobim had first taught her to swim, he had told her always to get in and out of the water quickly, for it was in the marginal moments—half in, half out of the water—that a person was most vulnerable to shark attack: It was then that the person looked truly like a wounded fish; most of the body was out of the water so it appeared smaller, and what remained in the water (lower legs and feet) kicked erratically and made a commotion like a struggling animal.

She spun, grabbed the gunwale with both hands, hoisted herself out of the water and over the gunwale, and tumbled in a heap to the bottom of the boat. She lay there for a second, breathing heavily, then realized—with a surge of adrenaline that rushed through her arms and pooled warmly in her stomach—that Jobim hadn't followed her. Her mask was still on her face, so she leaned over the side and peered down into the water.

Jobim clung to the anchor line, and he turned with the shark as it circled. Again Paloma thought of dogs—two males, one an intruder into the other's neighborhood, circling each other, appraising each other, searching for weaknesses.

When the shark was at the most distant point in its circling pattern, on the far side of the boat, Jobim pulled the bag of fish from his shorts and dropped it. The bag sank slowly, yawing like a leaf falling from a tall tree, and Jobim waited until he was sure the shark had seen it. Then, as the shark started down after the bag, Jobim pulled himself aboard the boat.

They ate a lunch of mangoes and bananas and a slab of dried, salted *cabrío*, making sure to eat the fish first and the mango last so that the juice from the mango would wash away the thirst caused by the salt in the *cabrío*.

They did not speak while they ate. Paloma didn't know what to say. She was certain she was supposed to have learned something, but she didn't know what it was and she wanted to review everything in her mind before asking any questions. Jobim knew that Paloma was searching for the lesson she was supposed to have learned, and he wanted the experience to ripen in her mind before he explained it.

Jobim rinsed his fingers in the sea and said, "Were you afraid?"

"Yes," said Paloma, and then, worried: "Is that bad?"

Jobim laughed. "Of course not. I don't think there was much danger, but they're fearsome things."

"No danger?" Paloma felt almost disappointed.

"People aren't their normal food. If the water's clear and they can see you, and if you're not bleeding or dead, usually they'll leave you alone."

"Usually," Paloma repeated.

"Usually." Jobim smiled. "Now: Do you know what you've learned?"

"No. I know I learned that you don't know what

sharks are going to do. I *knew* those two were going to take the needlefish from the big one, and then they didn't.''

"Do you know why?"

"There's a reason?"

"I told you I was going to show you something about girls.'' Jobim smiled again. "The big shark was a female, a very young one. A little girl, as sharks go.''

"How do you know?"

"How do I know she's a female? It's almost as it is on people. On the male you can see what are called claspers. They secure the connection during breeding. The female doesn't have any. As for how I know she's young, she had no scars on her at all. That's as it is with humans, too: The older you get, the more weather-beaten and cut up and scarred you are. An old shark looks like Viejo. And an old female shark has even more scars, because during mating the males prevent the females from throwing them off by biting the females' backs.''

"How old was she?"

"I don't know. Three or four years, I guess. Nobody knows how long they live or what kills them. It's hard to imagine a shark dying of old age, but maybe it happens.''

"What were the other two?"

"Both males, both older. You saw the way they turned and ran when that young girl came at them.'' Jobim paused, knowing what was going through Paloma's mind.

She frowned and said, "It doesn't make sense.''

"Not to a human, because we've been taught all sorts of ideas about males and females and the natural order of things. Males are bigger and do most of the physical work and support the family and make the decisions and must be looked up to and obeyed because . . . because why? Because that's nature? No. Somewhere way back, there must have been a good reason to make the males dominant. Probably because they were strong and did the hunting. And when strength was all there was, the stronger you were, the more important you were.

"And that's true with a lot of animals—the bigger and stronger are the most important. With sharks, the females are almost always bigger and tougher and meaner. Sharks have a pecking order, just like the chickens at the house. You saw it right then. When there's food around, the biggest eats first and eats till it's full. *Then* the others get to feed, but always in the order of their size and bad temper. That's why you don't see males and females together very often: The males would starve to death."

"But with people," Paloma said, "females *aren't* the strongest or the toughest or the meanest. They're . . ."

"Who says?" Jobim cut her off. "Strong doesn't only mean biggest; the toughest isn't just the one who can smash something with his bare hands. Strong can mean smart and clever and creative. The toughest can be the one who knows how to survive without wasting energy, or how to swim from here to there against the tide without getting exhausted and drowning.

"Animals have to be what nature made them—big or not, strong or not. That's what sets their place. But people can set their own place. If they don't have one thing, they can make up for it with something else, with knowledge or experience. Do you understand?"

Paloma nodded.

Jobim knelt down beside her and spoke softly. The image of his brown forehead and black eyebrows and broad shoulders framed against the sunlit sky was engraved forever on her mind, the sound of his mellow voice reduced to a hoarse whisper was one she would recall whenever, after his death, she talked to him. "All I want to tell you, all I want today to teach you, is that there are no 'must-bes' in life. Nothing is inevitable.

"You don't *have* to cook the food and sweep the floor and have babies. You are a female, and that is a fine thing. You are a young female, and that is finer still. But the finest thing is that you are a person who can decide for yourself what you want your life to be. You will teach people to respect you for that. More important, you will respect yourself for that, and anyone who doesn't is a fool, to be pitied."

Never, after that day, had Paloma wished to be a boy. She had let her hair grow until it cascaded down her back. She had watched and felt with pride and fascination every change in her body.

A few months after Jobim's death, a big storm blew through, a *chubasco* as big, if not as sudden, as the one that had killed Jobim. (That one had given no warning at all. He had surfaced from a dive to find his boat bucking and heaving in mountainous seas. He must have tried to board it and been knocked unconscious by the motor or the boat, for when he was found dead on the beach, there was a big blue dent in his forehead.) This storm knocked every bush and shrub flat against the ground and lashed the island with blinding, stinging rains.

The first rumblings began in her body almost simultaneously with the onset of the storm, and the cramps seemed to her to be echoing the thunder. She was frightened briefly, for her first thought was that she was becoming violently ill. Then her fear melted into a vague apprehension. Miranda had not warned her about what would happen when the woman change began inside her, had mentioned it only in vague, embarrassed generalities, and had, finally, turned it over to God to deal with. Jobim had done what he could to prepare her, but he could not know what to expect, how she would feel, what exactly would happen to her.

He had prepared her well enough, though, so that soon she felt the comforting conviction that everything that was happening was natural and healthy and—she remembered his word—fine.

She wanted him to know what was happening to her, and how she was responding to it, that she was becoming a woman and was proud of it.

And so, though a squall was driving the rain in horizontal sheets and the wind was whipping around in cyclonic eddies, Paloma fought her way to her rock on the western tip of the island and stood on the rock, naked. She raised her arms to the sky, to Papa, and beamed up at him, radiant with life, and let the rain wash the blood down her legs and over the rock and into the sea.

VII

PALOMA DRIED THE last dish, then walked outside into
the still night.

For all her delight at being a girl—and her frequent
amazement at herself for ever having wanted to be
anything else—still Paloma often wished that she could
abolish the differences between herself and males. For
she was positive that it was this difference (in coin-
cidence with the absence of other girls her age) that
made it difficult for her to make friends.

The slightest hint, therefore, that Jo might be un-
dergoing some sort of shift that would make him
susceptible to friendship gave Paloma an injection of
hope that animated her as much as an adrenaline rush in
fright.

As she puttered around the kitchen, she had reprimanded herself for not being more receptive to Jo's new
attitude. He had been rather nice tonight, and she had

responded skeptically, had put him off. He had given a little something, and she had given nothing.

So she decided she would go to Jo's room, and if he was awake she would tell him that she had been mistaken, that tomorrow would be a good day to teach him to dive.

As she turned the corner around the house, she heard something that made her stop. She waited, then peered around the corner and saw Jo going into his room. He must have gone for a walk, she thought, and she started again for his room. But again she stopped, and this time she wasn't sure why; she knew she didn't want to go on. She was sensing a warning—nothing she could have articulated, but something very strong.

As she stood there, she chided herself for giving in to mystical nonsense. But no matter how foolish it seemed, she could not take another step.

After a few more moments, she returned to the house and went to bed, resolving to let sleep clear her head.

But sleep was a long time coming, for she was an unwilling witness to a pitched battle inside her head—between the half of her mind that wanted a friend and condemned her for being suspicious, and the half that cherished her independence and was suspicious of anyone or anything that might encroach upon it.

By morning, she had decided to give herself the day to settle the conflict in her mind, so although Jo was still being genial, Paloma did not let the mild guilt she felt change her plans.

She accompanied Jo and his friend Indio down the path to the dock, as she did every day. As he untied his boat, Jo said casually, "You want to come with us today?"

"What?" Jo had never invited her into his boat—not

for fishing, not for fun, not to gather firewood on one of the nearby islands.

"Manolo is sick."

"Sick with what? He was fine last night."

"I don't know. He says it's his stomach. If it is, I don't want him in the boat."

Paloma was tempted. If she could not make a gesture to Jo, at least she might accept his gesture to her.

But selfishly, she did not want to accept. She had never liked fishing, except with Jobim, and then it wasn't the fishing she liked so much as the being with Papa. Fishing was boring and tiring and painful, for the fishing line always bit through her fingertips and abraded the cuts with salt. Most of all, she disliked fishing because it was killing—for a worthwhile cause sometimes, she had to admit, but still, it was killing. She could not reconcile the communion she felt with the animals on the seamount with the sense of revulsion, of horror, really, she felt on seeing those same animals lifeless and colorless, heaped in the bottom of a boat.

But if Jo needed her help, if they were going to be friends, it would be petty of her to refuse.

"All right," she said.

"Oh." Jo seemed surprised. "I mean, only if you want to."

"If you need the help, I'd like to help."

"Yes. I see." Jo seemed to be searching for something to say. "I don't really need your help, though."

"But I thought Manolo . . ."

"Sure, but . . . I mean . . . Indio and I can . . . Manolo doesn't really . . ." Jo was blushing. "We can manage. I just thought you might . . . I know how you feel about fishing . . . I mean, all we do is kill stuff." Jo grimaced, as if the thought of dead fish nauseated him.

"I know," Paloma said, "but that *is* what we live on. It's time I got tougher about it."

"Okay," Jo said. "Good idea. Only today's not a good day."

"It isn't?"

"No. You said so yourself, remember? We've both got a lot of things to do."

"Yes, but . . ."

"We can manage. Really. You do what you have to do then we'll spend a couple of days together. Maybe more. Maybe one day you can teach me to dive and the next day I'll take you fishing. A deal?"

"Okay." Paloma shrugged. She didn't know if she should say something more. Was she supposed to? Were there customs about this? It had seemed so simple: Jo had asked if she wanted to join them today. More: He had suggested that she could help them, had seemed to be asking for her help. She had said yes, she was willing to help. And then everything had gotten complicated. He had withdrawn the invitation, or denied the request for help—whatever, he was now saying that he didn't want her along, after all.

Or, was he being considerate of her? That was what his voice wanted to convey—that he didn't want to be so selfish as to take her away from what she wanted to do. If that truly was his message, if he was being kind, then perhaps she could respond with a kindness, should convince him that what she had to do wasn't very important, that she would gladly put it aside to help him.

But maybe he had changed his mind. If so, she didn't want to force herself on him.

Was this what the beginnings of friendships were like? If so, then maintaining a friendship looked like a full-time job. It was probably worth it, though. The least she could do was learn the tricks and rituals and give it a chance to grow.

And no matter how confusing she found this morning's conversation with Jo, the important thing was that they were being civil to one another. That demonstrated that both of them were willing to try.

Paloma uncleated the bow line and held the bow of the boat away from the dock while Jo and Indio climbed aboard. Then she held the bow from swinging in the tide while Jo tried to start the outboard motor. He pulled the starter cord, and the wheels and gears inside the housing made a purring sound like a feeding cat. He pulled again, and the purring sounded more anxious, then stopped abruptly. Jo cursed the motor and banged on the housing with his fist. Then, with a sigh, he removed the housing and began to tinker with the insides of the motor.

Before, Paloma had watched Jo's rages against the motor with amusement. Now, for the first time, she felt sympathy for him. He knew motors as well as she knew fish—was at home with them, could understand them and talk to them and cajole them into cooperating. But while Paloma's friends flourished in the Sea of Cortez, Jo's friends, the motors, withered and died. This was as hostile an environment as any on earth to an internal-combustion engine. Salt corroded its innards, the sun burned out gaskets and hoses, sand clogged filters and destroyed lubricants.

And there were no expert mechanics, no replacement parts. When a motor broke, you either fixed it yourself, rebuilt the ailing part, or dismantled and cannibalized it for parts to fix some other motor. Paloma remembered seeing Jo spend endless hours with a knife and a piece of truck tire—the tire had been a fender that fell off the boat from La Paz. He had carved and created from the thick rubber a tiny impeller for the outboard motor's water pump.

No wonder Jo wanted to go away to school. He had a gift that was little more than useless here. There were a couple of outboard motors for him to work on, but nothing of size or scope or genuine challenge. He had no way of developing his gift, of honing his skills, of letting his talent earn him money and appreciation. He was like a wonderfully gifted surgeon with no one to practice on.

He took something off the motor, cleaned it, blew on it, screwed it back in and replaced the housing. Then he caressed the motor, said something threatening to it, turned the choke up high, and yanked on the cord. The motor gagged and protested its way to life with a belch of blue-gray smoke.

On other mornings, she would have tossed the bow line loose into the boat, leaving Indio to unsnarl it from the fishing gear. Today she coiled the line carefully and knelt on the dock and handed it to Indio and pushed the bow of the boat around the end of the dock into open water.

Jo headed east, and soon he and Indio and the boat were black silhouettes against the pumpkin sun. Jo waved, Paloma waved back. Then Jo appeared to speak to Indio, and Indio waved, too, which Paloma found curious.

Paloma went back to the house to fetch some food and a jar of fresh water. Today, for no good reason except to avoid an argument, she let her mother wrap a slice of salted *cabrío* and a tortilla in a piece of paper for her to take along with her mango.

Then she returned to the dock and got in her pirogue

and pushed off and paddled westward.

She did not look back, but even if she had, it was unlikely that she would have seen the figure squatting in the bushes at the top of the hill, who was tracking her through a pair of binoculars.

VIII

MANOLO, SUPPOSEDLY WRITHING with stomach cramps in his bed, had taken several precautions not to be seen. He had removed his silver sacred cross and his brass pinky ring so they would not flash in the sunlight. He had covered himself with leaves and branches. And the pocket mirror he had brought he placed face down in the dirt, until the time came when he would need it.

Now he watched as Paloma paddled toward the west. The heat of the day had not yet arrived, but there was still enough tumult in the interaction of air and water so that, when magnified by his binocular lenses, the atmosphere around Paloma's hat and paddle when she moved emitted a shimmer.

Paloma paddled for a while, then checked her landmarks, dropped her anchor, and held the line in her hands until she felt the iron set in the rocks. Then she put on her mask and fins and snorkel, slid her knife into her belt and slipped overboard.

Not until then did Manolo feel confident enough to step out of the bushes and hold the mirror to the morning sun and flash it twice toward the east.

Paloma cleansed her mask and blew through her snorkel to clear it. Then she settled down, with one hand on the anchor line, to survey the seamount from one end to the other. With her vision restricted by the sides of her mask and by the turbidity of the water, she could not see a large area at a single glance. In air, with her peripheral vision unhampered and the distances crisp and clear for miles, she could see about 140 degrees. Down here, she could see about 40 degrees with each look, and if she tried to see more, she was certain to miss something.

In practical terms, the difference was that, on the surface, she could see everything in the entire circle around her, all the way to the horizon, in a bit more than two looks. Down here, she needed nine full and distinct surveys to see the same circle, and the distance she could see was never more than fifty or sixty feet.

In the first section she concentrated on, she saw nothing but rocks. In the second, a few quickly flickering shadows told her that hammerheads were cruising near the bottom, the colors of their backs melded by the monochromatic seawater into the same mottled green-brown as the stony top of the seamount.

On a conscious level, Paloma was not looking for anything specific; she was doing what she did every day, looking over the seamount to see what was there. But a half-step deeper in her mind, Paloma was looking for the injured manta, hoping—not daring to voice the hope—that it had found its way back to the seamount.

As her eyes moved methodically on through the third,

fourth, and fifth sections, hope gave way to resignation: The manta was not there, would not be there, and she had been foolish even to think that it might be there. Mantas were open-sea animals. They cruised ceaselessly, following the food, making their home, like petrels, on the wing. They were not territorial, had no reason to return to a particular area. And even if this manta contradicted the rule and happened to be territorial, Paloma reminded herself, the treatment it had received from her the day before would surely have driven it away.

In the eighth section she saw a manta ray, but it could not be the same one. It was smaller; from here, it looked like a discarded black tricorn hat. She was about to shift her gaze to the last section of the seamount, but her eyes lingered, and then suddenly the scene beneath her took shape and she realized that the ray below *was* the injured manta.

It was distance that had deceived her. The ray was down very deep, and perspective that had told her the truth: Now she could see that small as the manta looked from up here, it dwarfed the terrain around it. Sea fans, half as tall as a man and much wider, looked like postage stamps beside the manta; a passing hammerhead looked no bigger than a spaniel. Also, as she stared down on the animal's back she could see a white slash behind the manta's left horn.

She guessed that the manta was hugging the bottom because there was less current there; the surrounding rocks and valleys would disperse the massive flow of water. And where there was less current there was less tug on the ropes that tore at the manta's already battered flesh.

The manta was hovering in a temporary shelter, where the sea did not aggravate its pain.

That presumed—Paloma checked herself—that a manta felt pain. Jobim had told her that some animals have no sensation similar to what people call pain. They sense, by instinct, danger, shock, loss of a limb or of a vital fluid—but not pain. For pain was only a human word for a human feeling. Yet Paloma knew for certain that this animal felt something akin to pain, something that signaled alarm and distress, because yesterday when she had tugged at the ropes in the wound the manta had behaved like a dog that has stepped on a bee.

Paloma also guessed that it was instinct that told the manta it could find shelter in a place of less current and that there was less current near the bottom. Like any animal in pain, humans included, the manta would seek a path of least discomfort. It would move everywhere, into deep water and shallow, close to the seamount and far from it, and where it was most comfortable it would stay.

All of which was fine, Paloma thought, but the manta's quest for comfort posed a problem: She could not possibly help the animal if it was determined to stay at sixty-five or seventy feet. She could make a breath-hold dive that deep, but she could not hope to stay long enough to accomplish anything.

On the surface—but more dramatically underwater—it is a basic truth that the more you attempt to do, the more oxygen you consume. A runner breathes harder than a walker because the runner is using oxygen faster and needs to replenish it faster. Underwater, there is no such thing as breathing harder: You have the oxygen you came down with, and there will be no more until you return to the surface.

The first time Jobim had explained that basic truth to Paloma, she had responded with a weary sigh, as if she felt he was insulting her intelligence. After all, it didn't take a genius to realize that there is no air underwater; that is why you take a deep breath and hold it when you put your head underwater.

Later, however, after she had dived many times to many depths and experienced the different ways her body responded to different activities and exertions and pressures and sensations, she knew what her father had meant. You had to know before you dived how far you were going and what you wanted to do. To change your mind at the last minute, far underwater, was to invite confusion, exhaustion, panic, and death.

Paloma knew, for example, that she could easily dive down to sixty or seventy feet if all she intended to do was wrap her legs around a rock and observe the creatures of the seamount—or, at the very most, kick or swim calmly from perch to perch. She knew how to read the signals her body sent her, knew when to respond by starting for the surface. But if she were to go to sixty or seventy feet and were, say, to see a bed of oysters ten feet deeper still, and were to force herself down and begin to hack the oysters free and stuff them in a bag, the signals for immediate ascent would come right away. Because she had gone deeper and exerted herself more than she had intended and had consumed oxygen that should have been left in reserve for the trip to the surface, the signals would already be too late.

She would start up—not in the relaxed, oxygen-efficient way she knew to be best, kicking gently and allowing her body's natural buoyancy to take her up, but struggling frantically, flailing with her arms, scissor-kicking, wasting even more precious oxygen. Long before she would near the surface, the ache in her lungs would change from a dull tightness to a sharp, stabbing flame. Her temples would stop throbbing and would instead thrum in an incessant screech of pain; she would be at the threshold, near explosion.

She would look upward and see a slab of water dozens of feet thick, and at some unknowable moment would realize that she wasn't going to make it.

Starved for oxygen, her brain would begin to shut down. She would lose consciousness. The next thing she would know would be determined entirely by luck.

If she was lucky, she would pass out close enough to the surface so that her head would pop free of the water before the breathing reflex commanded her diaphragm to draw a breath. And if she was even luckier, she would rise on her back with her mouth turned upward toward the air instead of on her stomach with her face in the water, so that when her head did pop free and the reflex did command a breath, she would breathe air. After two or three breaths, her brain, like an engine refueled and reprimed, would reignite her consciousness. She would awaken, and though there would be a blank in her memory, she would soon be fit again and able to resume swimming and diving.

If she was unlúcky, her body would try to breathe underwater. Her lungs would expand and inhale salt water. She would cough and gag and inhale and cough and gag and inhale. She would drown.

And when finally she did reach the surface, no one would be there to pound and press her chest and expel the water and breathe life back into her lungs. More and more brain functions would cease, until at last the critical ones that govern respiration and heartbeat would close their circuits forever. She would not awaken. And the next thing she would know would be whatever one knows, if anything, after one has died.

Paloma knew her limits, and knew that to try to help the manta where it now lay was well beyond those limits. So she floated on the surface and waited. The manta did not move, did not flap a wingtip or switch its tail.

Suddenly it occurred to Paloma that the manta was dead. Perhaps it was not hovering above the bottom but was lying *on* the bottom.

No, impossible. If it were dead, other animals would already be feasting on it. That was another of the facts of life: As soon as something died, something else began to eat it.

She recalled once seeing a goat slaughtered. The goat stood, passive and unaware, its tail and ears and lips twitching to keep the flies away. And the flies stayed away. Then the goat's throat was cut. It stood on its feet for a moment, bleeding to death, and must actually have died on its feet, for when at last it toppled over, and before its head had hit the ground, flies were gnawing at its eyes.

Animals knew when animals died, and as yet, nothing was feeding on the manta. So it couldn't be dead.

But it could be dying. Maybe right then, as Paloma watched, life was drifting away from the great animal. She felt helpless and frustrated and angry. She had to help, but she was too far away; she couldn't let the manta die, but there was nothing she could do. Maybe it wasn't dying. Maybe it was resting. Maybe . . .

She had no choice. She had to go down and see for herself.

She took her deep breaths and felt her lungs engage the rhythm of expansion and contraction, and when they were as empty as she could make them she slowly filled them to capacity, shut her mouth and dived for the bottom.

She pulled herself down the anchor line until she was

a few feet from the bottom, then released the line and swam over to the manta. It did not budge as she approached.

She saw at once that the manta was not lying on the rocks. It was hovering, as she had first assumed, evidently resting in a quirky swirl of water that flowed steadily over the top of the seamount and over its huge flat wings and permitted it to remain stable.

The manta was so still that it seemed frozen or hypnotized or in hibernation. Paloma swam beneath it—she wanted to look at its gill slits and be sure they were pulsing, however feebly, for that was the most reliable sign that the animal was passing water over its gills and extracting oxygen from it. The big round eye swiveled downward and followed her until she was out of sight beneath a wing.

Paloma swam under the entire breadth of the manta, and it was like being in a cave, for the giant cloak shut out all light from above and cast a blanket of black shadow on the rocks.

The manta's left eye tracked her as she reappeared and swam up over the horn and hung above it, looking down at the deep laceration, with the skeins of rope still floating out like asps among the shreds of flesh.

The wound did not look much different from when she had first seen it. There might be fewer ropes in it— she had removed a few, and a few might have fallen away—but those that remained were as solidly embedded as ever. There were no evident signs of healing. And the fact that the manta preferred to lie quietly, not to swim and feed, told Paloma that it was ill, and very weary. It had no way of knowing that it must eat in order to survive. Its instinctive impulses were weakening and fading.

Left alone, the manta would languish, and left alone

it would surely be. Only the whales and dolphins—the so-called higher animals of the sea—actively helped one another. Mothers helped their offspring to breathe, and protected them from predators; the well helped the sick; the young and vital helped the old and feeble; the males deferred in feeding patterns to the young and the females.

Animals on the order of manta rays, however, were solitary in maturity, and therefore, when they were less than healthy, they were very vulnerable. They helped themselves or they died—uncontrollable natural processes either cured or killed them.

Paloma had to surface, yet she lingered for one more moment, feeling indignation—at nature, at fate, at mankind, at fishermen, at whatever had caused this fine animal to be hurt—because the manta was triply helpless: It could not help itself, she could not help it, and nothing else in the sea *would* help it. At the last second before she kicked off from the bottom, Paloma impulsively wrapped her arms around the manta's cephalic fin—the dreaded "horn"—and pushed upward: In desperation, she sought to prod the manta into rising to a depth where she could reach it and do something to help. Then, with the drums pounding in her temples and the ache beginning to sear her lungs, she sped up toward the light.

On the surface she rested, waiting until her breathing had returned to normal and her pulse had quieted to a point where she could no longer hear it or feel it. For good measure, she waited a few minutes more until, from lack of exertion, she shivered: Her body had grown cold, and the shiver was its attempt to generate heat. Now she could dive again and exercise with no ill effect.

She put her face in the water and looked down. The

manta was gone. First she thought she must be looking in the wrong place. She lifted her head and searched for distant landmarks. Could the boat have swung at anchor, disorienting her? No. Everything was as it had been when she arrived.

She looked again, starting with the first sector, on the far right edge of the seamount, and moving methodically sector by sector toward the left wall that ended in the abyss.

The manta was nowhere.

As she had risen to the surface, it must have fled. Perhaps she had frightened it by grabbing its horn in her arms. But if so, why hadn't it bolted then? Perhaps it had behaved like an opossum—staying dead quiet while she was near and then as soon as she had left and given it what it regarded as a safe margin, it had dashed off to distant refuge.

Paloma felt remorse, condemning herself for driving the manta away, when suddenly the giant was soaring toward her, up from the depths like a black bomber flying from the edge of the gloom.

It passed fifteen or twenty feet beneath her as she hung on the anchor line, its wings rising and falling in lazy symmetry. It made a wide, banking circle to the right, ropes fluttering behind, and returned. Then it stopped, directly under Paloma's boat, no more than ten feet beneath her toes.

The pressure wave from the movement of the enormous body through the water made Paloma and her boat bob like toys in a tub.

Paloma did not know why the manta had left the bottom, why it had come into shallow water, why it had stopped beneath her boat. She was tempted, but refused, to settle for the easy answer she knew to be wrong—or, if not absolutely wrong, at least implausible and silly: that is, that the manta knew she was trying to help, that her gentle gesture on the bottom had somehow communicated something, and that the manta had responded like a pet or a child.

But while Paloma did know that all those reasons were not reasons so much as wishful thoughts, she determined to conclude nothing: The manta was there, and she had to try to help it.

She slid her knife from her belt, took a deep breath, and dropped down onto the manta's back.

She braced herself, prepared for the manta to burst to life and speed away, but it did not move. She gripped the lip of solid flesh between the horns and bent to the wound.

One long tail of rope fed out of the wound down the manta's back. The end in the wound was snared in a mess of knots. Gently, Paloma tugged on the rope. A foot or two more came free, and then it pulled tight. The hand that held the lip of flesh felt a shudder course through the manta's body—like a mild electric shock or a series of tiny tics. The shudder subsided, and the manta lay still.

Carefully, with the knife's razor point Paloma cut the rope away and probed the wound, snipping knots and snares, casting away bits of rotten flesh and pieces of soft and flaky rope.

Then, one by one, the alarms in Paloma's body began to sound.

She tried to ignore them all, for she feared that she was causing the manta such discomfort that when she left this time the animal would depart permanently. She did not want to pass out, but she was not afraid that she would: She could make it to the surface in two or three seconds, and she knew she would have much warning before she lost consciousness.

She received that last warning—a tingling in her fingers and toes, a dullness in her shoulders and thighs, a thick feeling in her mouth and throat. She swept down with her arms, scissor-kicked twice with her flippers, and broke through to sunlight.

She held onto the side of the pirogue and gagged and gasped and cursed herself for taking such a chance. But she was unhurt, and she had cut away a lot of the rope. If the manta was gone—well, she had done what she could do, and she hoped that that had been enough so the manta could survive on its own.

When she had rested, she looked down into the water. She expected to have to search for the manta, but it had not moved. It lay still at ten feet.

Paloma breathed deeply and held her breath and was about to plunge back down to the manta, when a new sensation registered in her brain.

At first it was a feeling—a weak vibration—but then, as she concentrated on it, it became a sound. It was a high, very faint buzzing or humming. Still holding her breath, she listened carefully, to make sure she wasn't hearing a sound from within her own head. Then she breathed, to let the sound of her breathing break the monotone of the buzzing, and held her breath again. It was still there; if there was any difference, the sound was a bit louder now.

Paloma knew that even though water was not a particularly good conductor of sound, underwater certain sounds were sharper, more audible, more emphatic than they were on the surface. Knocking two stones together, for example, was used as a signal, because if one diver shouted at another underwater, the voice died in his mouth, but if he clicked two stones together, the sound traveled clearly and far.

Whale sounds also traveled vast distances underwater. They were varied, high-pitched clicks and whistles, and when you heard them you often found that the chatty whales or porpoises were so far away that not only could you not see them underwater; you couldn't see them when you raised your head out of water, either.

Certain engine noises could be heard from a long way away. The big, deep-throated diesel engines—called "growlers"—sounded like an army of bears marching across a wooden floor. Usually, you felt a growler coming before you heard it. The turning of the huge propeller would affect the water pressure, and you would feel a thumping on your eardrums or a light tapping on your arms and back. Smaller engines that turned faster made high, buzzing whines.

Paloma did not know the science of why certain sounds traveled underwater and others didn't. She assumed it had to do with the quality of the sound, the kind of sound it was. A human voice made a sound that was weak and unfocused. Water dispersed it instantly. A whale's voice was sharp and precise, and it seemed to pierce the water.

Of course, how a sound registered depended a lot on who was listening to it. Jobim had once told Paloma that a human ear was about as efficient as a crystal-set radio he had put together from a kit when he was a boy. It received a very small portion of the signals that were racing through the air all the time.

"We think there is a great silence underwater," he had said, "but the sea is really a very noisy place."

"It isn't noisy," Paloma had insisted. "It's the quietest place in the world."

Jobim had not argued, but on his next trip to La Paz he had bought a dog whistle. He had blown it for Paloma; it made no sound.

"It's broken," she said.

Jobim took her hand and led her next door. Their neighbor's mongrel had had a litter of puppies three weeks earlier. There were six of them, and they were curled in a pile beside the exhausted mother. Jobim handed Paloma the whistle and said, "Blow it gently. They're just beginning to hear, and you don't want to hurt their ears."

Paloma thought this was a joke, and she took a deep breath and was about to blow on the dead whistle with all her might, when Jobim suddenly snatched it from her.

"I'm serious," he said. "Watch."

He put the whistle to his lips and let a feeble wisp of breath escape through it. Paloma heard nothing. But for the heap of drowsy puppies, it was as if a pack of cats had fallen on them from the sky. They struggled to their feet and scrambled over one another, whimpering furiously. They fought to wriggle underneath their mother, whose head was cocked, whose ears were up and whose throat rumbled with a growl of confused menace.

Jobim stopped blowing the whistle, and immediately the puppies relaxed. The mother looked around, decided that the high-pitched alien had departed, and dropped her head to the ground.

"The point is," Jobim had said as he took Paloma home, "just because we can't hear things underwater doesn't mean there aren't sounds underwater." Jobim paused, as if considering whether or not to say what he was about to say. Then he smiled to himself and shrugged. "The same is true with vision."

"What do you mean?"

"The eye is a receiver, too, like the television sets you see in the store windows in La Paz. They receive a kind of signal. Your eye sees a kind of light. But there are kinds of light that your eye doesn't see."

"It doesn't see them, you mean, but they're there?"

Jobim nodded. "Yes. Good for you."

"You mean there are things out there," she waved her arm, "things that *are*, and maybe things that are happening, and I can't see them?"

"Well . . . yes . . . I suppose . . . but no one really knows what . . ."

"I don't want to talk about it," Paloma had said flatly.

Jobim was about to laugh, but he saw that Paloma's jaw was set and her brow was furrowed and she was almost painfully grave, so all he said was "Are you sure?"

Paloma nodded. "It's like infinity. I don't want you ever to talk about infinity again."

"Why not?"

"It scares me and makes me cry."

"All right," Jobim said, and he had squeezed her hand.

Lying on the surface of the water now, listening to the high, buzzing sound, Paloma tried to recall if Jobim had taught her any tricks for judging how far away a sound was. Either he hadn't taught her, or she couldn't remember them, and in any case it didn't matter. She assumed the noise was coming from a boat, probably an outboard, passing in the distance, and if so, it would surely keep on going.

Paloma checked to make sure her knife was secure in her belt, then took her breaths and dropped down to the manta. She saw the big round eye swivel up as she approached and follow her until she had passed out of its range and settled onto the broad black back. As she let herself down slowly, she noticed that her knees were smudged with black. She touched the manta's flesh and looked at her fingers: It was black, too. The manta's protective mucous coating came off on her skin like a black stain.

She turned to the wound; there were very few ropes left, and she was able to reach them with the point of her knife. She removed them all and then, with her fingertips, swabbed at the bits of debris left in the wound. She had to force herself not to think of what it would be like to have someone poking fingers into an open sore of hers, for when the thought first crossed her mind, she nearly fainted.

But the manta did not give any signs of pain, did not flinch or shudder. Either the wound was so deep that it was beyond superficial nervous sensation, or such sensations didn't exist in the manta. Whatever the reason, Paloma was able to clean the wound and cut away all the dangling shreds of putrescent flesh.

The feelings in her head and in her chest told her that she still had some time—half a minute or more—before she would have to surface, so, using her hands as trowels, she began to pack the torn flesh together into the cavity of the wound, pressing it down as if to encourage it to adhere to itself and grow again.

It should have been a silent task, but the flesh as she slapped it sounded like THUCK, and her moving around caused her to emit squeaky streams of bubbles, and the pulse in her temples drummed ever more insistently. And all these sounds, when added to her intense concentration, obliterated the noise of the outboard motor as it approached overhead.

Now she had to surface. She pushed off the manta's back and swept once with her arms and kicked a few times. It was only habit that made her look up: Jobim had taught her always to look up as she ascended from a dive, to avoid knocking her head on the bottom of the boat.

When she did look up, she expected to see the surface or the sky. Instead, all she saw was Jo's face, peering down at her from the surface through a glass-bottom bucket, his grin distorted by reflection into a gargoyle's leer.

She recoiled, shocked, and looked again to make certain she hadn't imagined it. Then she saw Jo's fingers creep around the edge of his homemade viewing box and wave to her.

IX

PALOMA BROKE THROUGH the surface and reached up for the gunwale of her boat. Jo had put a line around her anchor rope, so they were moored together.

He was still looking through the glass-bottom bucket. "Mother of God! What a monster! How did you catch him?"

Indio said, "Let me see."

Paloma's heart was stuttering. She could hear it beat in her chest and feel it in her throat. She took a deep breath and tried to calm herself, for she had to be in control of herself before she could hope to deal with Jo and Indio and—looking so smug, sitting in the bow—the miraculously recovered Manolo. Her first impulse was to shriek at Jo, to lash out at him, for she felt betrayed, even violated.

There were three of them, however, and but one of her, and nothing would be accomplished by a display of rage, except that Jo and his mates would laugh, and she would feel even more humiliated.

"How did you catch him?" Jo asked again.

"I didn't catch him," Paloma said. "He's not caught."

"He's dead, then?"

"No."

Indio was looking through the bucket. "*Look* at 'em all! This place is a fish market! It's a gold mine!"

A surge of nausea swept through Paloma and made her dizzy. Though she still hung in the water, she felt beads of sweat form on her forehead.

"I told you," Jo said to Indio. "I knew she wasn't coming out here to study shrimps."

"You were right."

"You didn't believe me," Jo went on. " 'Let's stay here,' you said. A lot you knew."

"Okay, okay," Indio said. "I said you were right. I admit it. I take it back. Now let's get at 'em!"

As if on cue, Manolo threw a baited hook overboard and fed the weighted line through his fingers.

"Don't!" Paloma shouted.

Manolo laughed. "There are fish down there. Are you saying I can't fish for them? That's what fish are for. To fish for."

"You're wrong." Paloma pulled herself toward the bow of her boat. "You're not so important that God put *any*thing on earth just for you to kill."

With one hand, Paloma grabbed her anchor rope; with the other she reached back into her belt and pulled out her knife and slashed the line that moored the other boat to hers. The line was taut, for the strong tide wanted to pull the boat away, so the sharp blade sliced through the fibers so quickly that they made a popping sound.

Immediately, the bow of Jo's boat swung wide, tangling Manolo's fishing line in the limp mooring line, and the boat slid away down-tide.

Furious, Jo leaped to his feet, cursed Paloma, and yanked on the starter cord of his outboard motor. The cord came away in his hand. He cursed the motor, and cursed Paloma again, and the cord, and all boats, and the sea. He rewrapped the cord and pulled a second time, and the motor sputtered and died. He cursed spark plugs and carburetors and gasoline.

Paloma clung to her anchor rope and watched Jo teeter in the stern of his boat and nearly capsize. Then she saw a puff of blue smoke and heard the outboard roar to life and saw the boat swing in a tight circle and head back toward her. Quickly, she pulled herself aboard her own boat, for she knew that Jo's rages were sometimes blind and violent, and he was capable of threatening to run her over with his boat. She didn't believe he would actually do it, but he might hit her by accident.

Aiming directly at Paloma's pirogue, Jo kept his motor at full throttle until he was only ten or twelve feet from her, then cut his power altogether. His boat stopped six inches from Paloma's, and it caused a swell that lifted her boat and tipped it and almost spilled her overboard.

Manolo, cheeks livid with anger, whipped his bow line around her anchor rope and made it fast. His fishing line was wrapped in a tight spiral around the bow line. He tried to unravel it, but every time he freed a loop of fishing line, the loop behind it kinked and doubled. He took a knife from his belt and cut the fishing line and snarled at Jo, "If you can't make her behave, *I* will."

"Don't worry," Jo said. "I'll take care of her."

"Jo, look!" said Indio, who had put the glass-bottom bucket overboard and was surveying the seamount. "*Cabríos*. Dozens of them. And goldens! And jacks! Jesus, a million jacks!"

Jo looked at Paloma and said, mocking her, "Not much out here, eh? Not many groupers. Just the same old stuff. I knew I couldn't trust you."

Paloma was stunned. "*You* couldn't trust *me*? Who was it who said he wanted to learn to dive?"

"I do, I do."

"To study things, to learn about animals."

"I do."

"No. All you want to do is kill things."

"No," Jo said, and he grinned. "I want to kill things and *then* I want to learn things. When I can sell enough fish to get enough money so I can get out of here, then I'll learn things—in Mexico City."

Paloma took the knife from her belt again and moved forward toward the mooring line.

"Paloma," Jo said in a tone reminiscent of Viejo's martyr voice, "don't be so silly."

"Give up, you mean. Let you kill everything here."

"There you go again, exaggerating. Even if I wanted to I couldn't kill everything on this seamount. If we take something, something else comes in to replace it. The sea goes on forever, you ought to know that."

"That's nonsense. You could wipe out the whole place."

"I'm not going to argue with you, but . . . what do you care, anyway? We won't take your precious oysters."

"What? I . . ."

Jo smiled. "Didn't think I knew, did you?"

What does he know? Paloma wondered. He can't know about the necklace. He can't. He'd spoil it. If he knew, he'd find some way to spoil it, just to get back at me for . . . for what? For succeeding where he failed?

Paloma stalled. "Knew what?"

"That you take oysters from here. You're so pure, you never take anything from the sea, sure, sure. Well, I've seen oyster shells in your boat." Jo chuckled. "Or that thing you call a boat." He looked around and was pleased at the appreciative smiles from Indio and Manolo.

"A couple of oysters," she said, relieved, and she added for emphasis, "to eat right here. That's all."

"That's what we want: a few fish to sell. That's all."

"Jo . . ." Paloma hesitated before continuing. "Papa wanted this seamount saved, left as it is. He told me we had a kind of trust, that we had to preserve it. It . . . it was his favorite place."

Jo flushed. "I know that. You think I didn't know that?" The words spilled from his mouth. He turned to Indio and said contemptuously, "Of course I knew that. You heard me say that."

Indio looked quizzically at Jo, but said nothing.

Then Jo glared at Paloma and shouted, "Papa is dead, Paloma! Dead, dead, dead!"

She put her hands to her ears, for she did not want to hear.

"I don't care if he told you to save the whole world! He is dead, and what he said doesn't mean a damn! Do you understand that? Not a God damn! It is what I say that makes a damn, and I say I am more important than your stupid fish!"

There was nothing more Paloma could say, and so she raised her knife to cut the mooring line.

"That won't stop us."

"Yes it will. I'll pull my anchor and go. You'll never find this place again."

"I'll buoy it."

"I'll cut your buoys away."

"I'll take landmarks."

"You?" Paloma sneered. "You couldn't find your way around the house with a landmark. You don't know how."

"I can learn."

Paloma knew he was right. He could learn to take landmarks, and once he had the skill, he could find the seamount as easily as she did.

"Look, Paloma, we don't have to fight like this." Jo was trying to sound reasonable. "We can work it out. We can still be friends."

Paloma had been looking away from him. Now her eyes snapped back to his face, to see if he was purposely mocking her. He was looking intensely sincere.

He said, "I'll make a deal with you."

"What deal?"

"I won't tell anybody about this place. It only makes sense that I'll keep my word; after all, it's good for me, too. We'll fish it with lines only, no nets. Anything we catch that we can't use, we'll throw back."

Paloma saw that Jo's mates were eying him as if they thought he had lost his mind, but they stayed silent.

"You have to admit that's fair," Jo said. "I don't *have* to do anything. I could come out here and throw dynamite overboard."

"You could," Paloma agreed. "But you know that if you did"—she hoped her voice had a tone of quiet menace—"I'd get revenge. Somehow, someday, you'd pay."

Jo roared with laughter and slapped Indio on the back, but there was a brittle quality to his laughter, for Paloma was—physically, at least—an unknown and thus an unmeasurable adversary. He was bigger and stronger, but he seemed to sense that she was quicker and smarter, and driven by a passion that gave her courage.

Paloma thought about Jo's "deal" and concluded at once that it was no deal at all; it was a not-very-subtle kind of blackmail. If Paloma agreed to let them fish as often and take as much as they wanted, they would not spoil a good thing by spreading the word to their competitors. If she harassed them by cutting away their bait and their boat and their buoys, they would broadcast the location and its richness.

Worse still, Paloma doubted that they would be able to keep their end of the agreement. It was inevitable that one of them would find himself in a conversation in which he needed something to brag about, a feat that would set him apart from and above his rivals. And once the existence of the seamount was known, its location would follow speedily.

It was also inevitable that before long Jo and his mates would begin to fish with nets. The temptation would become too great to resist. It would be like placing a plate of Easter sweet rolls before the three famished boys and recommending that they eat no more than one apiece because there would be no more when that plate was gone. They would see huge schools of *cabrios* and jacks beneath their boat, and each flashing body would ring in their minds as a silver coin. They would be catching four or six or fifteen fish on their lines, and they would begin to speak of the immense fortune that was swimming away from them because they could not use nets. Then they would agree to try the nets just this once, to see how many fish they could catch—an experiment, they would say, that's all. They would catch hundreds and hundreds, and there would be no satisfying them with less. The seduction would be complete.

They would tell each other (and believe the words) that fishing with nets was fine and just, because God had given man dominion over all the animals.

"What about it?" Jo said. "Do we have a deal?"

Suppose she said no. Suppose she declared open war on them. It was possible that she could make their days on the seamount so miserable that they would leave. It was more likely, though, that their response would be to confide in a few of their friends and bring two or three more boats out with them. Paloma would be overwhelmed. They would begin to use nets; life on the seamount would end even sooner. She had no choice. By agreeing, she might buy time.

"Okay."

"Smart," Jo said. "Very smart." Like a military commander ordering his troops to advance, Jo gestured at Indio and Manolo, telling them to start fishing. Obviously, he was enjoying himself enormously: He was the leader who had negotiated a favorable truce that exploited his enemy's weakness, and now he would deploy his forces to reap the rewards of his wisdom.

Paloma watched as Indio and Manolo baited hooks and dropped their weighted lines overboard. She put on her mask and leaned over the side of her boat and looked down into the water.

The manta was still there, still immobile, ten feet below the surface. The fishing lines passed four or five feet in front of the manta's left wing. If the manta were to decide suddenly to leave, and if, as usual, it gained momentum by slowly raising and lowering its wings and gradually flying forward, its left wing would collide with the fishing lines. It might brush them aside and proceed unharmed. But if the wing were to strike the lines solidly, and if there were tension from above and below—preventing the slack that would be needed to permit them to buckle and slide aside—the lines might slice through the flesh. Or they might lodge in the flesh, as the fisherman's nets had, and bite deeper and deeper as the manta struggled.

The injury would be similar to the one Paloma had just treated, but more severe, for the thin monofilament line could cut through the flesh and, perhaps, even amputate part of the wing. The outcome then would be certain death.

Paloma put on her flippers and slipped the snorkel through her mask strap.

"Where're you going?" Jo asked.

Manolo called out, "Stay away from my line."

"Don't worry," Jo said to him. "We made a deal. She knows she better not fool with me."

Paloma said nothing. She rolled over the side of her boat, breathed deeply, and dived to the manta. She checked the wound and saw that the flesh she had packed in was staying firm; it had not begun to unravel and shred. Perhaps it would heal and grow. Without the constant abrasion of the ropes, probably it would not get worse.

There were no predators or parasites nearby, which told Paloma that the manta was not emitting distress signals. Its mechanisms must be gaining confidence of survival. And that made her feel good.

What the manta did not need, however, was a new injury. So, after Paloma had examined the wound and patted it and gently stroked the flesh around it, she hovered above the furled horn on the right side and reached down and pressed on it. She wanted to guide the manta, and since it had responded once before to her touch on one of its horns, she was guessing that the horns were as sensitive as a horse's mouth and that the manta would react to pressure on its horns by moving in a way that would relieve the pressure.

When the manta did not respond at once, Paloma pressed harder, bending the horn toward the bottom. She felt a shudder as, somewhere deep in the core of the giant, a message was received, almost as if a command had been given for the boilers to be stoked, the engine to be started, the vessel to be moved. Silently, the right wing dipped, the left wing lifted, and together they heaved once up and down. The pressure pushed Paloma away and forced an explosion of bubbles from her mouth. When the bubbles cleared, she saw the manta bank to the right and keep rolling, like an airplane in a spin, as it flew toward the bottom.

Jo had watched this through his viewing box on the surface. Now, as the others held their lines, he took up a honing stone and began to rub it in tight circles against the point of a harpoon.

"What are you going to do with that?" Manolo asked.

"The deal just said no nets."

"But what you gonna stick?"

Jo gestured at the deep water where the manta had gone. "He'll be back."

Manolo whistled. "*There's* a few pennies."

"I *told* you I'd take care of you."

"You did?"

"Sure. Remember? I said all you had to do was tell me where she'd gone, and I'd take care of the rest."

"Oh."

"You two stick with me and we're going to be fine," Jo said, smiling. "Just fine."

Below, Paloma watched the manta swim toward the

bottom. It was on its back, showing its brilliant white underbelly, and as it arrived at the rocky top of the seamount it continued its slow and easy roll, spinning and descending, like a child falling down a sand pile, until the black of its back became one with the dark water of the abyss and Paloma could see it no more.

She wanted to follow it, to roll with it down the side of the seamount, to make discoveries with it and be part of the harmony of the sea.

Instead, her body sent her signals that told her she was very much a human being and that if she intended to continue to be a live human being, she had better ascend.

On her way up, she continued to look down, happy that she had been able to help the manta, hoping that it would survive, sad that in order for it to survive it would probably have to stay away from this seamount that was no longer a sanctuary, and—struck by this last realization—suddenly very angry.

At the distant limit of her vision, something was moving, thrashing violently. For a second, Paloma thought it was the manta—perhaps it had snagged a fishing line, or been attacked by something—but then the animal was drawn a bit closer, into her field of focus, and she saw that it was too small to be the manta.

Then, as it drew still closer, she could see that whatever it was was struggling to return to the bottom, fighting something that was forcing it to the surface. Because she had never seen such sights on the seamount, it was two or three seconds before she realized what she was watching: a fish caught on a hook, being dragged up to the boat.

And then the fish was only a few feet from her, struggling less and rising fast, and she saw what it was and felt a rush of bile into her throat: a triggerfish—exactly like the one, perhaps exactly the one, she had seen valiantly defending its egg cache.

Impulsively, she put out a hand, hoping to grab the line and free the fish, but she was too far away, and before she could move closer, the fish had passed her. She looked up through the last three feet of water between her and the surface and saw the fish, limp now with exhaustion, splash into the sunlight and disappear into the shadow of Jo's boat.

She reached for the side of her own boat, broke through the surface and spat out her snorkel, and, choking, shouted, "Put it back! Quick!"

Manolo looked at her as if she were mad. "What?"

"Throw it back!" Paloma gasped. "You don't have much time."

Manolo looked at Indio, and they smiled and shook their heads at one another.

Manolo said, "I've got all the time in the world."

"But . . . you . . ." The words were a jumble in Paloma's mind. Thoughts crossed over thoughts, and they all bunched together and blocked each other out. She wanted to, *had* to, tell Manolo that the triggerfish must be returned to the water immediately; that in less than a minute the sun would begin to harm its skin and cause ulcers; that in only two or three minutes, the fish would asphyxiate, for it could not draw oxygen from air; that it was probably already in some kind of shock from the struggle on the line but that it might survive if it could get back into the soothing salt water *now*.

But in spite of all she wanted to say, nothing came out of her mouth except, ". . . you don't understand."

Again Manolo smiled, and what should have been obvious to Paloma all along now struck her like a blow to the head: It was *she* who hadn't understood. And what she hadn't understood was that Manolo had no intention whatsoever of returning the triggerfish to the water, that he regarded the triggerfish as fairly caught and rightly his, and that he would consider anyone who tried to prevent the fish from dying in the bottom of the boat to be a thief.

Now that she did understand, she could say only, "But why?"

"Why what?"

"You don't eat that fish. Nobody eats triggerfish."

"Cats do."

"*What?*"

"Grind it up, make pet food out of it. Very nourishing." Manolo held up the twitching triggerfish and whinnied, "Here, kitty . . . here, kitty." Then he dropped the fish back into the bottom of the boat.

"But . . . but . . . that beautiful thing," Paloma sputtered. "You'd waste its life for . . ."

"What waste? Get a lot of 'em, they pay for 'em." Manolo reached for another piece of bait on his hook.

Paloma knew better than to argue; it would be a waste of time—not only her time, but the fish's time. Every second she spent trying to save it, it was dying.

"Throw it *back*!" she screamed.

Manolo gazed at her, and there was no expression in his eyes. "Okay," he said. "You've convinced me."

He reached into the bottom of the boat and picked up the triggerfish by its tail. He pretended to examine it for a moment, then said, "Looks a little faint. Better wake it up." He swung the fish high and slammed it down on the gunwale of the boat. The sleek body, once purple and gold, now mustard and dull gray, shivered once and was still.

Manolo looked to Indio, who was grinning, and said, "That didn't work. I don't get it." Then he turned to Paloma. "You know so much about fish. Here. You try.'' And he threw the fish across the water.

It landed in front of Paloma and splashed water in her face. The flat body floated on its side. The fins did not flutter, the gills did not pulse. The eye, which in life was a black so vivid that somehow it manifested fear and fury, calm and curiosity, was now as flat and dead as a porthole into an empty room.

Paloma held the corpse, to keep it from drifting away in the tide. She said nothing, for there was nothing she could say that would make any difference—certainly nothing that could change what had already happened, and probably nothing that would change what was going to happen.

She looked at Manolo, who was baiting his hook and glancing furtively at Indio for approval, and at Jo, who had been looking at her but quickly shifted his eyes away as soon as he saw her looking at him. Now he pretended to be deeply concerned about a knot in his fishing line.

Jo is trying not to look embarrassed, Paloma thought, but he *is* embarrassed because he has no real control over these others. Even he wouldn't be stupid enough to pull a stunt like Manolo's so soon after trying to appear reasonable. But he could not stop Manolo— would not have tried to stop him, for Manolo would have told him to stick a fish hook up his nose and pull out his brains, and Jo's self-image as commander-in-chief would be exposed for what it was: basically a fraud, tolerated by the others for only two reasons—the boat (which had been Jobim's) belonged to him, and he had engineered the deception that found Paloma's sea-mount.

In a way, Manolo had done Paloma a favor. Like a deft surgeon with a sharp knife, he had excised from Paloma a tumor of softness, of gullibility, of desire to be liked, of willingness to trust. Like one of the ancient pirates who used to sneak up on his victims flying a friendly flag and then, at the last moment, break out his pirate banner, Manolo had shown their true colors.

Without a word, Paloma reached behind her for her knife. Swiftly, she cut the triggerfish in half, then in quarters. As soon as blood began to billow in the water, the tiny sergeant majors materialized and searched in frenzy for the meal that must be there.

Paloma let the pieces of triggerfish fall one by one, and through her mask she watched each one as it was consumed by the swarming sergeant majors.

She felt numb doing this, as if somehow she was compensating for the evil that Manolo had done, restoring a natural balance that had been upset by his brutality. He had killed an animal and would have let it rot in the sun until it could be ground into powder—an end that denied the animal's life any dignity. She had at least achieved a disposition that was cleaner, quicker, and more natural. Forget that the triggerfish had died at the hands of a pig. Its body was now being returned to its home, serving to nourish the other creatures of the seamount, and prolonging the life of the community.

The blood dispersed and became part of the sea; the pieces of fish descended into the mists, shrunk to nothing by the frantic nibbling of the little fish that, from here, looked like clustered bees. Only the bones would reach the bottom.

Paloma climbed into her boat and removed her mask and flippers. In the other boat, all three were now fishing, and they did not notice her as she went forward and tugged at her anchor line to shake the killick loose from the rocks below. The killick was well caught, and Paloma had to bounce the rope several times, pulling it this way and that, hauling it tight and giving it slack, to force the iron to shift position and work loose. At last, she felt an easing of the strain on the rope, and when she pulled now, it came up at a steady pace.

Free of the rocks, Paloma's boat drifted off the seamount. Moored to Paloma's boat, Jo's boat drifted with it.

Jo was the first to sense that something was wrong. The others' lines were already down; they had been hanging within a couple of feet of the bottom. When the tide carried the boat, it carried their lines as well, so they felt no difference. But Jo was just letting his line down when the boat came adrift. He waited for his hook and sinker to strike bottom, but they kept falling, for by now the boats were away from the seamount and over a bottom that was four thousand feet away. Jo's line fell and fell, and the deeper it went the faster it fell, until his entire spool of line was all but empty.

He turned and looked at Paloma's boat in time to see her pull her killick aboard and cast his boat away from hers. He shouted, "Hey!"

"I have to go home," Paloma said calmly. "Put down your own anchor." Then she knelt in the pirogue and raised her paddle.

"But where's the bottom?"

"Right there," Paloma said, pointing vaguely to a spot in the sea a couple of hundred yards away. "You can't miss it. Not a fine navigator like you."

The others were already hauling in their lines, and Jo rushed to bring his aboard. He shaded his eyes and squinted at the shore, hoping to recall landmarks barely noted when he had approached the seamount. He started the outboard motor and put it in forward gear at half throttle and aimed it against the tidal flow, reasoning that to recapture the seamount all he would have to do was reverse the direction of his drift.

"Put the bucket over," he ordered Indio. "Tell me when we're there." They had not been drifting long, so he assumed he would be directly over the seamount within a few minutes.

Indio put the glass-bottom bucket over the side, then gripped it tightly with both hands, for the movement of the boat against the strong tide tended to tear the bucket from him. All he saw below was blue.

"Well?" Jo said impatiently.

"Nothing."

"You got to be wrong."

Indio looked up from the bucket. "Kiss a goat. Look for yourself." Indio snickered and added, "Mister fine navigator."

Jo put the motor in neutral and took the bucket from Indio. The tide caught the bow of the boat and swung it wide to the left and pushed it half a circle around, then struck the stern and pushed it after the bow: Slowly, the boat was drifting in circles. Jo paid no attention. He stared through the glass-bottom bucket at the endless carpet of blue beneath him.

"Impossible!" he said.

Manolo smiled. "A miracle!"

"God's will!" chimed Indio.

"Shut up!" Jo said. He brought the bucket aboard and put the motor in gear and gave it full throttle. The boat lurched forward, rose to a plane, and traveled several hundred yards before Jo got his bearings and turned the bow against the flow of the tide. He continued up-tide until he judged he had compensated for his movement sideways, then stopped and told Indio to look again.

"Nothing."

Manolo said, "I think you're way off to the side."

"I can't be," Jo insisted.

"You could be above it," Indio suggested. "You traveled long enough."

"No. Did you see how far we drifted?"

Manolo said to Indio, "There's only one thing for sure: He doesn't know his butt from his bucket about where he is."

Jo said, "You could do better?"

"I couldn't do worse."

Manolo looked at Indio, who looked at Jo and shook his head and murmured, "What an ass."

Jo was confused. His command was unraveling, and he could not deal with sniping from two people at once. And so he focused on one, on Indio, and said, "Get out."

"Get out of what?"

"The boat." Standing in the stern, Jo pointed at the sea. "Get out of my boat."

"And what?" Indio said, laughing. "Walk home?"

"I don't care. It's my boat, and I say get out!"

"And I say"—Indio mocked his imperious tone—"go suck a lemon!"

Jo took a step toward Indio, Indio grabbed the bulwarks on either side of the boat, the boat yawed dramatically, Jo lost his footing and started to fall overboard. To save himself, he twisted in mid-air and fell across the motor. The motor was hot, and Jo yowled like a scorched cat and pulled his hands away from the motor and lost his balance and rolled into the water. He hit head-first and went under for a second and came up sputtering and clawing for a hand-hold.

Indio guided his hand to the side of the boat and said, feigning concern, "What'd you do that for? You always tell me you don't like swimming."

Jo gurgled and sputtered and tried to utter a threat, but all that came out was drool.

"If I were you," Manolo said, "I'd get back in the boat."

Jo struggled to haul himself aboard and then lay panting across the after thwart. He scowled at the other two, and hated them for forming an alliance against him, hated them for seeing through him, hated them for making fun of him, hated everything because there was nothing he could do about anything. Except . . .

Jo shaded his eyes and stood up and looked across the water. Far away and moving still farther, appearing from this distance no bigger than a piece of driftwood, was Paloma's pirogue.

If she hadn't cast them loose, none of this would have happened. They would not have lost the seamount, and, in trying to find it, Jo would not have suffered the collapse of his authority. All he had left to give him superiority over Indio and Manolo was his boat, and that was not enough. They could always find someone else with a boat.

What he hated most about the collapse of his façade was that he had been so careful, so meticulous in erecting it. By being extracautious on the sea, he had assured that his seamanship had never been tested; by staying in the same fishing spots, he had never had to try his nonexistent navigational skills; by announcing that he wanted to learn to dive, he had scored points for courage, while knowing full well that once he had stolen from Paloma the secret of her seamount she would never agree to teach him anything.

He didn't care about the respect of others except insofar as it encouraged them to help him reach his goal—the acquisition of enough money to leave this island and get away from this wretched sea and into a city, where life depended on the function of mechanical things that he could create and care for and repair.

Here he was a misfit, and he knew it, but he had survived. Until now. With a single thoughtless gesture, Paloma had destroyed his credibility with Indio and Manolo. The only way to restore that credibility was to destroy its destroyer, to prove once and for all that he was stronger, more worthy, than Paloma. And such a proof would settle more than the matter of the moment: It would avenge the humiliation he had felt when his father had replaced him with a girl.

He would bring her to her knees before him. She would acknowledge his superiority, beg for his mercy, promise to obey him, and . . . He would think of other things when the time came.

Jo turned and yanked on the motor's starter cord. The motor caught at once, which he took as a good omen, and he pushed the throttle open and spun the boat around.

"Where are we going?" Manolo asked. Pounded by the thumping bow, he half stood, letting the muscles in his legs absorb the strain.

"She's gonna put us back on that seamount," Jo shouted above the noise of the engine.

Indio said, "I bet we could find it ourselves."

"If we had a week," Jo replied. He poked a finger at Indio's chest. "Every minute we're not fishing that seamount, she's costing us money. She's costing *you* money. You want to go to La Paz and fly on an airplane and see things and meet people?"

"Yeah. You know that."

"Then blame her that you're stuck here." Now he pointed at Paloma's pirogue, which was growing larger and closer every moment. "She's the one got you chained to the island; she's taking the money from your pocket."

"I never thought of that."

"Well, think of it. Because we're gonna stop it right now."

Paloma was more than halfway home when she heard the outboard bearing down on her. Immediately she sensed Jo's mood—if not his precise intention—because the engine noise broadcast an unmistakable message: Only someone ignorant of boats or out of control would run an engine at full speed in the open sea. It was dangerous to the sailors and damaging to the engine. Jo knew boats. The engine pitch was at peak hysteria, and so too, Paloma sensed, was Jo.

It had probably been a mistake to cast Jo's boat loose, for she had known he would soon be lost. He had never learned how to interpret tides and currents, couldn't differentiate the subtle shades of blue and green that would tell him how deep the water was and what kind of bottom was below. What she could not have known was how vulnerable he was, and how quickly his embarrassment would change to rage.

Paloma stopped paddling and waited, for there was no point in trying to outdistance him. She wondered if there was anything she could say that would defuse him. The engine noise came closer, a shrill and painful scream. She looked up and saw the white hull rise out of the water and slam down, spewing rooster tails of spray from both sides of the bow. The boat was aimed directly at her.

Still she waited, now shaken by a new possibility: Might he actually ram her pirogue? Could he be *so* stupid? He might sink the pirogue, true, but he would certainly damage his own boat as well. She wondered if she should jump overboard and go underwater and wait for him to pass. But then he might take her boat. Besides, it was a cardinal rule that you never abandoned your boat unless it became absolutely . . .

They were upon her.

The white bow rose over her and came straight at her, and for a split second she thought she would be crushed. Then, suddenly and violently, the bow skewed off to the left and she had a flashing glimpse of Jo's face and the shrieking motor before a mount of water struck the pirogue and lifted it nearly vertical. Paloma threw herself against the far bulwark, against the lean of the boat, and it righted itself and settled into a trough. Quickly she steadied herself and stood up to see where Jo's boat had gone. She had to know where he was so she could see him if he came at her again.

The boat was thirty or forty yards away, turning in a tight circle, running over its own wake, caught in criss-cross patterns of swells and chop, the motor spewing smoke and screeching as the propeller bit through pockets of air instead of water. Manolo stood in the bow, bracing himself with the anchor rope, his head thrown back, laughing. Indio sat amidships, steadied by an arm pressed against each bulwark. And Jo knelt in the stern, turning the boat and aiming it once again at Paloma.

This time he turned away a second sooner—Paloma was able to keep the pirogue from capsizing simply by shifting the weight in her knees and balancing with her hands—and then he stopped. His boat wallowed a couple of feet away.

"Get aboard," he said, indicating his boat.

"Why?"

"You're going to take us back to that seamount."

"Find it yourself."

"I'm not asking you; I'm telling you. Get aboard!"

Without thinking, Paloma raised a hand and ticked the thumbnail off her front teeth at Jo. As soon as she had done it, she knew it had been a mistake, for the rude gesture compounded the effect of her refusal: It showed not only defiance but contempt. Jo blushed, and Manolo and Indio exchanged snorts of amazement, for neither of them had ever seen a female make that gesture to a male. It was beyond insolence; it was unthinkable.

Jo put his boat in gear and turned away, and Paloma could see the veins in his neck protruding thickly. He drove the boat perhaps thirty yards, then turned again toward her.

"One last time," he called to her. "Will you take us back to the seamount?"

Silently she shook her head.

"Yes you will. I gave you a chance to do it the easy way, but if you want to go the hard way, that's okay with me."

She heard his engine yowl as he revved it in neutral, and she knew what he intended to do. He wanted to capsize her, to separate her from her pirogue so that she would have to beg him for a ride, and he would pick her out of the sea only if she would take him to the seamount.

But she would not give in, would not surrender the seamount, would not betray herself and her promise to her father just for the sake of putting money in Jo's pocket. If he wanted the seamount, he would have to find it himself and take it himself. She knew that eventually he would find it, but it would not be with her cooperation. Meanwhile, for as long as he wanted to upset her pirogue, she could keep it upright by balancing with her hands and knees. Soon enough he would get bored, or decide that he had made his point, and he would go away.

Then she saw the oar.

His boat was directly in front of her, his bow facing

hers. He always carried two oars, in case his motor died and he had to row home, and now he had fit one into an oarlock and had directed Indio to hold it horizontal, so that most of the hardwood shaft stuck straight out from the side of the boat and the oar blade was turned so its sharp edge faced straight ahead, straight at Paloma.

Again Jo gunned his engine in neutral, the way an airplane pilot does before takeoff to make sure the engine will give maximum power at the critical moment. Together, Jo and his boat seemed to be some strange monster pawing the sea, preparing to charge.

Now, for the first time, Paloma felt genuine fear, for she knew she had badly miscalculated. She was no longer dealing with Jo, but with a mindless, violent creature who had surfaced only once before and whose single appearance had finally and irrevocably ruined Jo's relationship with his father.

The scars caused by Jo's panic underwater had healed. Jobim had not only forgiven him but had even come to regard the episode as his own fault for having pushed Jo too hard. Jobim had taken Jo's training back a few steps and had proceeded more slowly, more gently.

They had still been a team.

It was late summer, in a lull between the migratory cycles that mark the end of one fishing season and the beginning of another. Every year at this time, the islanders had a fiesta. It was an ancient festival that had been going on since well before Viejo's memory, must have gone on even before the time of the Spaniards, for some of the masks that some of the children wore represented old gods (their names long since forgotten) that lived here before the Christian God.

The centerpiece of the fiesta was a fishing tournament. Anyone could enter and could fish with anything he wanted—hooks, harpoons, spears—anything except nets. The winner was the fisherman who returned with the most weight of fish.

Jobim had entered the tournament every year, and every year he came in last. He had no interest in prizes, no need for public approval, no fondness for catching masses of fish. What amused him about the tournament was the challenge of trying to catch fish in ingenious ways, ways that gave the fish a more-than-even chance.

One year he fished without a boat and with barbless hooks. He swam out to the nearest shoal and fished with bent pins. He hooked several fish, most of which straightened out his homemade hooks and fled. With his last hook (a huge safety pin), he snagged a big grouper and, by playing it with infinite patience and care, brought it to the surface. Only then did it occur to him that he had no way of getting his fifty-pound prize to shore. So he removed the safety pin from the lip of the grouper and turned the exhausted fish around and pushed it back down into deep water.

Another year he had used a boat but no fishing gear. He anchored his boat and surrounded it with chum—a savory blend of tiny baitfish and guts and blood. The chum attracted schools of jacks and legions of sergeant majors and a dozen groupers and a few sharks, all of which swarmed around his boat. Jobim's challenge that year was to catch the fish barehanded, as a bear does in a stream. His trophies at the end of the day consisted of countless puncture wounds in his palms, caused by his grabbing fish by their sharp dorsal spines, and one mangled fingertip, souvenir of a grouper who had mistaken his finger for a bit of chum.

This particular year he had entered the tournament with Jo as his partner. They were going to fish underwater, using spears Jobim had fabricated by copying a picture he had seen in a magazine. The spear was a steel rod, propelled by a rubber sling attached to a wooden sleeve.

Perhaps with long hours of practice a fisherman could learn to be accurate with one of these spears, but Jobim had finished making them the afternoon before the tournament, so he and Jo had been able to practice for only an hour or two.

The balance in the sling was precarious: Usually, the spear skewed away too soon and shot up or down or off to the side. Or the spear skidded and slipped on its way out of the sleeve, and plopped listlessly and harmlessly out and down. Or Jo held the sling wrong, and it slapped so hard against his wrist that it left an angry red welt.

Though he had never dared say so to his father, Jo desperately wanted to win the tournament, for he felt he needed a badge of accomplishment to give him stature with his friends. He had hoped that by fishing underwater with his father's invention, he would have an advantage over the competition. Now that he saw that the invention wasn't so marvelous, however, he was distressed.

"I'll never hit anything with that," he had said. "We don't have a chance."

"Probably," Jobim agreed, unaware of the significance that Jo was attaching to the tournament. "But we'll have fun. Most people only *use* the sea; we *enjoy* the sea."

But Jo didn't enjoy the sea; he wanted to get out of it what he could, and be done with it.

By midday, he and Jobim had caught nothing. There were plenty of fish around, but neither of them could hit a thing. Every time Jobim missed, he would moan underwater and pretend to tear his hair and then would laugh and dive to retrieve his spear. Every time Jo missed, he cursed bitterly. Finally, he left his father alone in the water and returned to the boat.

All around them, other fishermen were hauling fish aboard their boats. Nearby were some of his friends, with their fathers, and when they saw that he had caught nothing, they taunted him for being incompetent and for obeying a father so foolish as to try to catch fish by sticking them with a steel rod.

Jo felt the blood rushing to his face and pounding in his neck, and before he knew what he was doing he had leaped to his feet and cocked his spear and unleashed it at the nearest boat. The spear had clanged harmlessly in the bow of the boat, but it had scared the fishermen enough to drive them away—shouting angry threats at Jo.

And then Jo—frantic now beyond reason to prove that he was a winner, the best, that even if his father was strange, Jo himself knew how to get things done—pulled a small bag from a cubbyhole beneath a thwart. He had never thought he would have to use this bag, didn't know what would happen if he did, but he was glad he had brought it along, for the situation called for extreme measures.

The bag contained firecrackers—the big, canisterlike ones with the waterproof fuses—bought in La Paz for the fiesta and stolen by Jo from the common store.

Now he would show them who could catch the most fish. The firecrackers would explode underwater, so no one would hear them. Stunned fish would float to the surface. He would gather them up, pile them in his boat and later stick them with his spear to make it seem that he had caught them. It didn't occur to Jo that there was anything wrong with this stratagem: devious, yes; tricky, yes; clever, certainly. But wrong? The rules said only, no nets. Jobim might even admire his ingenuity.

Jo lit one of the firecrackers and threw it overboard, from the side of the boat away from where he had last seen Jobim's shadowy form underwater. As he watched it sink and waited for it to explode, he wondered just how much damage a little explosion like that would do to a fish.

He never thought to wonder what it would do to a man—until, after he had heard the muffled WHUMP, he saw his father thrashing, struggling toward the surface and saw the clouds of blood streaming from his ears.

When Jobim's head had broken the surface, there had been a moment before his eyes rolled back and he fainted from shock and pain. In that moment his eyes had locked on Jo's, and in his eyes were accusations of stupidity, recklessness, and cowardice.

Jo had screamed, "I'm sorry! I'm sorry!" over and over, but no one had heard him.

Now, waiting for Jo to charge at her again, Paloma knew that the same kind of switch had been tripped again in Jo's head. Whether a reservoir of restraint remained within him she could not tell, but, for the moment, she was faced with an irrational animal whose fury was being fueled by encouragement from his unthinking mates.

With the engine in full throttle, Jo reached back and flipped the gear lever from neutral into forward. For a second or two, as the pitch of the propeller blades changed and they sought to grip the water, the boat moved not forward but down. The bow rose, then fell, and the boat was up on a plane, flat on the top of the water.

He was determined to capsize her, and so intense was his obsession that until he succeeded he was prepared to hurt her or maim her or perhaps even kill her.

She had resisted so far by counterbalancing. But if she could not use her knees and hands, if she were forced to lie on the bottom of the pirogue, a weight as immobile and unsecured as a sack of grain, when a wave struck the boat and lifted one side high out of the water, her weight would roll to the other side and destroy the boat's natural balance and force the high side to keep rising until, finally, it passed the point of no return and pushed the boat upside down.

What frightened her was not the thought of capsizing, but the knowledge of how Jo intended to compel her to lie on the bottom of the pirogue. At full speed, he would sweep the pirogue with his extended oar, from bow to stern. If Paloma stayed on her knees, balancing with her hands, the oar would strike her in the stomach. If she ducked down, it would strike her on the top of her head or her back, for the pirogue was so shallow that she could escape the oar completely only by lying flat.

If she didn't duck quite far enough, or if she lifted her head in an impulse of resistance to capsizing, the oar would hit her in the neck or the face. In this last second, as her eyes focused only on the oar and saw it as a scimitar, she thought of flinging herself overboard but decided against it because she knew it would deprive Jo of the satisfaction he craved. *He* had to do something *to* her.

So she threw herself forward onto her face and covered the back of her head with the palms of her hands and braced her elbows against the sides of the pirogue.

She never saw the oar, never heard it, but she felt the puff of pressure wave that it pushed before it as it swept the pirogue, and she felt the oar's blade nick the pirogue's wooden sides and bounce and nick again.

Then the wake of the motorboat slammed into the pirogue and heaved it upward. Paloma was no longer on her face, but on her side, then over on her back, and then there was only grayness and a hollow slapping sound and she was under the boat. She stayed there, breathing the air trapped beneath the boat, trying to get control of herself and guess what, if anything, Jo planned to do next.

The engine noise told her that the motorboat was moving away and that Jo had throttled back. She heard incoherent voices, talking calmly, and then the engine noise grew louder again. The boat was returning, but slowly this time.

The engine noise dropped to the low mutter of idling speed, and she heard the wavelets lap at the motorboat's hull as it wallowed.

"Where is she?" Indio's voice filtered into the chamber where Paloma's head stuck out of water. He sounded worried.

"You've drowned her!" said Manolo.

"She's not drowned," Jo said. "I'll show you where she is."

Suddenly Paloma's ears were battered by a sharp, metallic clang that echoed from side to side of the wooden cavern. Jo had hammered something—what, she could not imagine—against the upturned bottom of the boat.

"Hey!" he called. "Ready to take us to the sea-mount?"

Paloma did not reply. Partly, she didn't know what to say, didn't know what another flat refusal would goad him into doing. But partly, too, she hoped that by remaining silent she might scare him—even briefly—into believing she had drowned.

"I knew it!" came Manolo's voice. "She's dead!"

"No," said Jo, but there was a lilt of uncertainty in his voice, a hint of fear. Again the metal thing struck the bottom of the boat, but softer than before. "Paloma!" he called.

"Paloma!" Indio shouted.

"Leave it to me!" Jo snapped at him. And then Jo took a gamble: "Paloma, I know you can hear me. In my hand is a harpoon. If you don't agree to take us to the seamount, I will punch a hole in the bottom of your boat with my harpoon. Your boat might not sink, but it won't paddle, either, so you will stay here and float with it till kingdom come . . . or you will take us to the seamount in return for a ride home. Your choice."

The harpoon dart dug at the boat, and Paloma heard the steel point grind into the wood fibers. It might take him time to dig a hole through the bottom of the boat, but there was no doubt he could do it. And if the hole was big enough, the pirogue would behave exactly as he said: It would wallow awash and drift with the tide.

She had to surrender; it was the only reasonable thing to do. But why should she apply reason to a situation that had so far been completely irrational? Jo hadn't used reason in what he had done. Why should she? So she stayed beneath her overturned boat, listening to Jo's labored breath as he gouged a hole in its bottom.

First she saw a pinprick of light, and then a shaft the size of a coin, and wood splinters fell on the water before her. Then the head of the harpoon jammed through the hole and turned a couple of times and was withdrawn.

"There!" Jo's shadow crossed the hole and disappeared. "Good-bye, Paloma. You may think you're being proud, but all you are is pigheaded."

Paloma heard Jo pull on the starter cord of the motor. The motor sputtered but did not start.

"We can't leave her," she heard Indio say. "We have to make sure."

"Sure of what?" Jo said. As he talked, Paloma felt herself growing cold, not from the water but from the icy logic oozing from the mouth of this person who was her brother. "Make sure she's under the boat? Make sure she's all right? Why? Suppose she isn't. What are you going to do about it? Nothing. When we get back to shore, we say we have no idea where she is, which is the truth because we don't. You don't talk about it to anyone because you know that if you do I'll come for you. And you believe I mean what I say because I do."

Listening to Jo, Paloma realized that he had accomplished at least one of his goals: He had restored a certain stature to himself among his peers. He could not be different or special by being better or more skillful than the others, so he had set himself apart by being reckless, unpredictable, dangerous. If he could not make them respect him, the next best thing was that they should fear him.

"But believe me," Jo went on, "she is under the boat and she is all right. She will come back to shore and she won't talk about what happened because she'll be too embarrassed, and besides, no one can do anything about it and probably wouldn't believe her anyway, and if she does talk a lot and complain to our mother I'll get her sometime, and she's like you—she knows I mean what I say and she better treat me better than she has."

Paloma heard the outboard wheeze and jump to life, and she could feel through the water that Jo had put the motor in gear and was driving away.

X

SOON SHE COULD no longer feel the faint tapping in the soles of her feet, the sensation caused by the tiny shock waves emitted by the turning of the propeller. She guessed that the boat was already about a hundred yards away.

She wondered whether she had been right or wrong, smart or foolish, principled (as she believed) or pig-headed (as Jo had said). At best, she had delayed Jo a few days. He would find the seamount eventually and do his damage, perhaps destroy it. And the delaying tactic had cost her . . . what? She couldn't even guess yet. Here she was in the middle of the sea, with the end of the day approaching and no way to get home unless she could devise some way to patch the hole in her boat.

But futile though her gesture might prove to be in the long run, it had been the right thing to do. Jobim would have approved. He would have told her that she had

struck a blow for life. And she knew that to strike such a
blow himself, he would have gone to almost any extreme.

Once or twice, he *had* gone to extremes. She recalled
now a story he had told her about an incident he
described as one of the most important, and dangerous,
of his life. He was telling her, he had said, to teach her
that there were times when you had to take big risks
over matters of principle. And he had sworn her to
secrecy because if the truth were ever to surface, it could
start a war between Santa Maria and some of the other
islands in the Sea of Cortez.

Late one summer, the fishermen of Santa Maria had
discovered that one of their prime fishing grounds—a
deep seamount in open water far from shore—was fast
becoming barren. Every day it was more difficult to get
a fish on the line, and what few fish there were looked
scruffy and battered.

Their first thought had been that one of their number
was using nets, but it was pointed out that huge nets
were impractical in such deep water. None of them had
a boat equipped with the powerful electric winches, the
wide cockpit, and the support structures necessary to
handle the nets.

Then they had concluded that some water-borne
plague was killing all the fish. Every now and then, the
depths of the sea would spawn and spew up clouds of
poisonous microorganisms that contaminated hundreds
of thousands of fish—either making their flesh toxic to
human beings, or killing the fish themselves. But again,
someone pointed out that if the fish were being killed,
they would float to the surface and be seen, and if the
fish were being made poisonous, surely by now people

would be aware of someone falling sick or dying, either here or in La Paz.

So it had to be something else, something new and strange and alarming. A few people insisted that it was God's way of punishing the fishermen for being careless over the generations, for taking too much too indiscriminately.

Jobim knew that it had nothing to do with God. As usual, people were turning to God because He was a quick answer for unanswerable things. The more Jobim saw and heard, the more he smelled the scent of man.

Contributing to the fancies of the other fishermen was the fact that not one of them had ever seen the top of the seamount. None of them dived, none knew anything about what underwater terrain actually looked like. They assumed that fish lived somewhere down there, waiting, presumably, for the chance to bite a baited hook.

But Jobim had seen seamounts, if not precisely this one, and he knew what to look for, and so one afternoon he had paddled out to sea and anchored. Even if he hadn't already known why he had never dived on this seamount, his anchor line would have told him: The killick dropped straight down and shot past five fathoms, past ten fathoms, past fifteen and eighteen and twenty fathoms (the last marked spot on the anchor line) and stopped, at last, at twenty-two fathoms—132 feet.

Jobim could not dive that deep. No one he knew could dive that deep. In fact, as far as he knew, no normal person could breath-hold dive to 132 feet. To dive that far would be like crawling down a tower made of two dozen men standing on one another's shoulders, or like falling from the top of the tallest building in La Paz. There would be no bottom visible for more than half the way down, and when and if you got more than half the way down, from there you wouldn't be able to see the surface.

But Jobim knew enough about his own capabilities to be willing to try—not to go all the way, but to go far enough so he could see the bottom. So he hyperventilated and sped hand-over-hand down the anchor line, toward the blue-black mists, through the gloom where there was no up and no down, until he could see the top of the seamount far below.

He went farther, waiting for the body signs that would tell him to stop, and before they came he had been able to see enough to need to see no more. From 90 or 100 feet he had seen most of the top of the seamount, and the landscape told an obvious tale.

The soft corals and sea fans were lying on their sides, ripped up by their roots like a tree in a *chubasco*. Many of the hard antler corals were broken into small pieces among the rocks. The vegetation of most of the bigger rocks was covered with a layer of sand. One brain coral the size of a bathtub was split in two, and its halves lay in a sand valley like slabs of melon.

There were fish—a few small ones darting in and out of the rocks, and a good-sized *cabrío* that looked healthy until suddenly it flipped over on its back and swam in frantic circles, and one moray eel, dead and wedged into a crevice as if by a swift surge of tide.

The seamount had been devastated by a series of quick, terrible storms whose force had killed nearly every living thing and had maimed the survivors.

Had nature sent the storms, Jobim would have been sad. But he knew they were caused by men, and he was angry.

Fishermen from another island—Santu Espiritu, a

few miles away—must be coming here at night and tossing overboard sticks of dynamite with long waterproof fuses. Long fuses were for the protection of the fishermen: A fuse too short would burn down too fast, and the dynamite would explode too close to the boat, cracking open the bottom and perhaps sinking the boat. But long fuses were a disaster for the seamount: They burned all the way down to the bottom, so the dynamite exploded not in open water (where its concussive force would kill the fish in the immediate area) but among the rocks and sand and coral, where pressures would build and channel and spread, killing animals in their dens and destroying the seamount itself.

Underwater, dynamite was a much more terrible weapon than it was on the surface. In air, a stick of dynamite—not packed in anything to contain and amplify the explosion, like rock or cement, not covered with anything to shatter and become shrapnel, like glass or pebbles—wouldn't do much damage beyond about ten yards. It was said that the detonation of a single stick of dynamite underwater could be felt more than half a mile. It could cause havoc over an area of thousands of square feet.

After the explosions, the fishermen would spread nets on the surface and scoop up the corpses of the animals as they floated up from below.

This was a quick, economical, and final kind of fishing. No risk of damage to expensive lines and hooks. No need for baitfish. Everything on the seamount was killed instantly. No time-consuming wait for a fish to bite. Best of all, the fish came to the surface on their own; you didn't even have to pull them up.

It was efficient and illegal and universally condemned as immoral, sacrilegious, and self-defeating, for every-

one knew that it destroyed fishing grounds and could
only hasten the day when whole communities would be
forced by starvation to become (the ultimate nightmare
of them all) beggars on the streets of Mexico City. Even
the worst louts among fishermen considered dynamite
fishing beneath contempt.

But Jobim knew enough about certain kinds of
people, about how stupidity and brutishness and greed
could combine to drive a person to do things that even a
moment's rational thought would perceive as destruc-
tive, to self as well as others. It was the promise of great
profit at little expense and no risk, of quick money in
the hand right now and don't worry that there won't be
any more when the fish are gone. Someone else can
weep over that. I'll get mine while I can, and other
people can worry about themselves.

It was the same mentality that led the company that
made fertilizer in the city to pump its chemical wastes
into the harbor. The company got rid of its wastes,
which was economical and good. The government, however, began to think that it wasn't a good idea to keep
pumping chemicals into the harbor where people swam
and fished, so it told the company to stop.

The workers had rioted and tried to burn down the
government building, because they said the company
couldn't afford to haul its wastes elsewhere, and if it
had to do so, some workers would lose their jobs and all
would lose an impending raise in pay. The government
backed down; the company continued to pump wastes
into the harbor.

Two and a half years later, the harbor died. The
chemicals had formed a poisonous sludge that coated
the bottom and choked all the vegetation and shut off
the oxygen in the water and killed every living thing.
Guests at the luxury hotels, who swam in the harbor,

began to come down with ghastly skin ulcers.

The government ordered the hotels to close and told the chemical company to stop pumping chemicals into the harbor. But the chemical company had made no plans to haul its wastes elsewhere, and so, compelled to stop using the harbor, it closed down.

Because there were no longer any hotels to stay in or restaurants to eat at or waters to swim in, the tourists and vacationers stopped coming to the city, and all the gift shops and boutiques closed and pitched their workers into the streets.

The workers at the chemical company had gotten their raise in pay, and for a few months had enjoyed the money. But because of their insistence on that new money they had lost everything. And it was not just they who were punished, but all the other workers who had lost their jobs. And eventually, "all" became everybody, for the city was deprived of a reason to exist, and slowly but inevitably it ceased to exist.

Nowadays it was a dusty cluster of empty buildings in a ring around the still-dead harbor, with the skeleton of the chemical company standing on a promontory as a reminder to passersby of the fragility of things.

But such lessons were hard to learn and easy to forget, and right then, over that seamount, Jobim had proof that some people still hadn't learned. Almost everyone in the islands had a cousin, or at least an acquaintance, who had chosen quick and easy money at one time or another. Perhaps he had sold the fishing boat his father had left him and taken the money to the city where he intended to go into business for himself, not realizing that he was already in business for himself, the business for which he had been trained and at which he was as good as any in the world. And when he got to the city he found that it was already full of businessmen who were all too eager to relieve him of his money (which was certainly not enough to start a new business anyway), so very soon his money was gone and he was begging for a job cleaning toilets in the city comfort station and smelling, instead of fish and sea air, ammonium chloride that burned the lining out of his nose.

But those people, everyone's cousin or friend, harmed only themselves and their families. These men from Santu Espiritu threatened to destroy the livelihoods of everyone on their own island, on Santa Maria, and on all the other islands as well. For they would not stop until they had cleaned out every seamount, every fishing ground they knew of, had heard of, or could find.

And Jobim knew what they would be saying to themselves, how they would be justifying behavior for which each of their mothers would have spat on them. They would say to one another, and hear one another say in reinforcing response, until they all believed it: If we don't do it, somebody else will; people are no good, and the only ones who survive are those who look out for themselves, and survival, after all, is what life is all about.

Jobim would stop them, but he would have to do it alone. If he alerted other Santa Maria fishermen, and they all went out in boats and waited for the raiders from Santu Espiritu, the raiders would see their boats and would flee. There would be a chase and a fight, and a lot of people would be hurt. Or, if the raiders escaped to Santu Espiritu, they would deny everything and accuse the people from Santa Maria of making up stories to cover their own misdeeds. There would be a long and bitter fight between the two islands in which everyone would be hurt except perhaps those who deserved to be. And they, meanwhile, would be out at night in new places, destroying life on new seamounts.

So Jobim made a special trip to La Paz and went to see a boyhood friend, a man whose father had received and sold the fish for Jobim's father many years ago. The friend worked in a salvage yard, where ships and boats and machines and cargoes and all sorts of other huge metal things that had been raised from under the water or saved before they could sink were brought to be restored or cut up for scrap.

Jobim and his friend had a beer, then two, and while his friend kept saying (time and again but in different words) that he envied Jobim for being able to be his own man and work at his own pace and live his life on the sea instead of in a place where the noise and the dirt were enough to drive a man crazy, Jobim kept asking questions about the newest methods and tools of salvage—especially about new ways of separating metals underwater, things like hunks of steel or parts of ships.

He said, finally, that a ferryboat had sunk near Santa Maria and was becoming a nuisance to the fishermen because it kept snagging and tearing their nets. The ferryboat was too big to move, but he thought that if he cut it into pieces, perhaps he could tow the pieces into deeper water where they would be out of the way. Would he need to hire underwater welders to do this? Would his friend's salvage company do the job for him? Of course, he couldn't pay much, but . . .

"Thing like that, you wouldn't cut it up," said his friend.

"Oh?" Jobim had known that all along, but he was trying to lead his friend into giving him more information without his friend's knowing why—in case what Jobim had planned went wrong and any part of it was ever traced back to his friend.

"You'd blow it up. The new stuff we use cuts sharper

than a knife and a hundred times quicker than a torch. You mix it, prime it, set it, fire it and POW! The job is done.''

"What is this stuff?''

"They call it PLS. It's a liquid, *two* liquids. You carry it in two separate jugs till you're ready to use it, because once it's mixed it starts to generate heat and if it gets too hot it goes off by itself.''

"How much would I need to blow up a ferryboat?''

"Depends how big the ferryboat is and how many pieces you want it in.''

Jobim described his imaginary ferryboat. It was old and ratty and not too big, and it hadn't been carrying anything of value when it sank. He wanted to be sure there was nothing about this boat that would be of interest to a salvage company. "How much do you think your company would charge to blow it up?'' he asked when he was finished.

His friend shook his head. "We wouldn't touch a small job like that.''

"I didn't think so. This . . . PLS . . . you talk about, is it hard to use?''

"Easy. Anybody can do it, long as they're careful.''

"Even me?'' Jobim smiled.

"Someone good with his hands as you? A snap.'' Then his friend saw where Jobim was taking the conversation, and he said, "But there's a problem.''

"Where can I get some?''

"That's the problem. You can't. Have to have a license for it. It's what they call unstable, and they don't want just anybody to have it and leave it lying around.''

"How much would I need?''

"From what you say, a couple of gallons. Say, a gallon of each of the two parts. But you might as well want a ton. You can't buy it.''

"Your company . . . wouldn't have any extra . . ."

His friend shook his head. "If we did, we couldn't sell it unless you get a license."

Jobim didn't know what to ask next. To keep the conversation moving, he said, "That ferryboat is costing a lot of people a lot of money. It's taking food from the mouths of children."

"I wish I could help you. If we were caught, we'd lose our business."

"Of course," Jobim had said. He didn't want to push too hard and put his friend in a difficult position. "You don't have any you could just . . . spill for me, do you?" He smiled again, to show his friend he was joking.

"That stuff you don't spill," his friend said with a laugh. "There's no such thing as extra. After a job, what's left over we have to throw away."

"Where do you throw it?"

"In the sea."

"Where in the sea?"

His friend waved his hand toward the water. "Right out there. Off Cabo San Juan."

Jobim lowered his voice. "How far off?"

"Not far. Maybe a hundred yards. At the edge of the shelf."

"How deep is the shelf?"

"Fifty, sixty feet. A lot of the stuff falls over the edge, though."

"Some doesn't, I bet."

"I wouldn't know."

"You throw it away mixed?"

"No. It could go off. It's in its separate elements."

"In cans?"

"In plastic bottles."

". . . that don't rust."

His friend nodded.

Jobim looked at the height of the sun in the sky and said, "I have to get back on this tide." He stood and held out his hand to his friend. "It is good to talk with you."

Shaking hands, his friend said, "One more thing, just for your . . . interest: The plastic bottles are different colors. It takes one red and one white to make a whole . . ."

". . . a whole pink one."

Jobim stopped at a store where they sold hardware and electrical parts. Then he returned to his outboard motorboat and made sure that both his gas cans and his freshwater jug were full, because the trip home could take anywhere from six to eight hours, depending on wind and tide. He told everyone at the dock that he was heading straight for Santa Maria, and he took messages from cousins for cousins, from friends for friends.

At the mouth of the harbor he turned right, which was the way home, and waved one more time. The people on the dock waved back and as far as they were concerned he was gone, which was true, although he stopped for a few minutes for a couple of quick plunges off Cabo San Juan.

For the next two days after he got home, Jobim stayed ashore and tinkered. He scavenged things from here and there and built things from this and that and endured all the teasing from his neighbors about how the schools of *cabríos* and jacks were running thicker than ever. People wondered what he was doing, and they asked delicate questions that hinted at the basic question—"What are you doing?"—but they never asked that outright. They all knew Jobim well enough to be aware that he permitted them to know about him only those things he wanted them to know.

Usually, when he was involved in an eccentric project,

he let slip information little by little, and saved the final result as a surprise—at which everyone would either marvel (if it was a success) or laugh (if it was a splendid failure). When he failed spectacularly, he laughed harder than anyone. But, in front of children, he made sure they realized that failure was just as important as success because you had to fail in order to know that failure wasn't worth fearing. If you feared failure, you would never try difficult things, and trying was more important than failure or success. (It was a lesson Jo persistently refused to learn: He loathed risks and was frightened by the unknown.)

This time, Jobim let slip no information about anything. He acknowledged only that he was working on some silly notion that was doomed to failure but that had preyed on his mind for so long that he had to play it out to its conclusion.

One night after supper, he told Miranda he was going for a walk, and he disappeared into the twilight. Much later, all anyone would remember was that they were positive they hadn't seen him again that night. He hadn't taken out his boat, that was certain, because many men were down at the dock cleaning fish and sewing nets; he hadn't been entertaining the neighborhood children, because people recalled that that was the night they had taken turns ministering to the little girl who had been stung by a scorpion; and he hadn't been in his own house until just before dawn. As far as anyone knew, he hadn't been anywhere. (He confessed to Paloma that he had enjoyed causing the mystery; it added spice to the otherwise predictable daily routine of the island.)

In fact, he had gone to the opposite side of the island—uninhabited, wind-burned, rocky, dotted with little puffs of the hardiest vegetation—where there was no lee in which to keep a boat or build a house or even pass a moderately comfortable night.

He skidded and scrambled down the steep slope. About three quarters of the way down, he stopped at a hole in the rock face and tore away the branches he had stuffed into its mouth. Inside was a large plastic garbage bag and a wooden platform about three feet wide and six feet long, to the bottom of which had been attached, with bolts and ropes, four old automobile-tire tubes.

He dropped the platform the last fifteen or twenty feet into the water and, with the plastic bag slung over his shoulder, hurried after it and climbed aboard it. He positioned himself on his knees, at the exact center of the raft, with the plastic bag tucked between his legs. Like a surfer on a board, he began to paddle away from the island.

He had picked his night carefully: It was flat calm, so paddling was easy, and there was no moon. There was just enough of a ground swell so his little raft would not be visible in the starlight: An observer's eye would be accustomed to a gently moving horizon; something as small as the raft would blend in. The timing and direction of the tide were exactly as he wanted them.

It was after ten o'clock at night when he arrived at his destination, a spot of water in the open sea, to most eyes no different from any other spot of water in the sea, but to his at the precise juncture of imaginary straight lines drawn from three landmarks faintly perceived—more sensed than seen—by the light of the stars.

From the bag he took a line and a killick. He dropped the killick overboard and waited for it to set in the rocks on the seamount. He checked his drift and the amount of anchor line left and decided that he had ample play: He could pull himself up-tide, or let himself drift down-tide, over a distance of a couple of hundred feet.

From the plastic bag he took two gallon jugs, one red and one white. He poured half of each overboard, on opposite sides of the raft, which was a silly caution but one that gave him comfort. Then he poured the contents of the white jug into the half-full red jug, and screwed the cap into the red jug. The white jug he returned to the plastic bag.

The cap of the red jug had been prepared ashore. A hole had been drilled through it, primer cord fitted through the hole and sealed. The primer cord looked like thin plastic clothesline, which was essentially what it was, except for the fact that it was filled with a substance like gunpowder that burned much hotter and many times faster.

To the other end of the primer cord Jobim had connected, by electrical contacts, a hand-powered generator. You squeezed it, and squeezing it turned some wheels that squirted power into the primer cord.

He lowered the full red jug into the water. If it had been empty and open, the plastic jug would eventually have filled and sunk. But filled now with a liquid of approximately the same density as water, and capped off with a bit of air trapped inside, it floated. Its neck bobbed, and the white primer cord waved back and forth, very visible against the black water.

Jobim didn't want the jug to float on the surface. He wanted it to have enough negative buoyancy so that it would tend to sink and yet be able to be held close to the surface by the tension of the tide working against the primer cord. The tide would try to pull the jug down and away; the primer cord would hold it up and near, and Jobim could pull in or let out more cord until he had the jug suspended where he wanted it—four feet below the surface.

So from the plastic bag he took a handful of pebbles, and he dropped them into the red jug and recapped it and tested it and put more pebbles in and tested it again until, finally, it was right.

And then he lay on his stomach on the raft, and he waited.

With nothing to do but wait, he worried. He worried first that he had thrown away too much of the PLS liquid, that the combined gallon he had saved wouldn't answer his purpose. But if his friend had said two gallons would blow a ferryboat to bits, surely one gallon would do for this job. After all, he was not trying to replicate World War II.

Then he worried that he had too much of the liquid, that it would do too much damage. Maybe he ought to . . .

Just then the light breeze brought the sound of voices. There were men approaching, and they were not being careful to keep their voices low. They had no fear of being overheard, this far out to sea. The only precaution they had taken was to paddle rather than use their motors, for they knew that the sound of a motor carries for miles in still air across still water.

Jobim lay quietly on his raft, his head down so he would make no silhouette against the night sky. He heard four distinct voices separated into two distinct pairs: two boats, traveling together but keeping a convenient distance from one another.

So far, he had guessed right: There had to be more than one boat, because to spread and gather the net from one boat would take so much time that dead fish floating on the surface would begin to drift out of range. A third boat, on the other hand, wouldn't contribute much but would add risk: The more people who knew about these expeditions, the more chance there would be that someone would talk too much. Besides, the fewer partners, the larger each partner's share.

Now, Jobim guessed, the two boats would stay close together. One would drop an anchor, and the other would moor to the stern of the first boat. They would check the drift and ready their nets, and then they would throw the dynamite—probably one stick off each side. The dynamite would explode so deep that all they would feel up here would be a weak thump of pressure on their wooden hulls. Then the anchored boat would feed out the net, and the other boat would drop back and drift with the tide, dragging the net, and paddle in a wide circle, returning finally to the anchored boat.

After a few minutes' wait, all that would remain would be to draw the net tight and haul in the fish and fill their boats and paddle home.

The voices drew closer, and still Jobim heard the sounds of paddles swirling through water, and he knew he had made a terrible error: By picking what he regarded as the ideal spot, he had picked the exact spot they were coming to. They were going to paddle into him, or at least into his anchor line.

Then what? At worst, depending on who these people were, Jobim would find himself in a fight for his life against four men, all carrying knives as an item of clothing and who had sticks of dynamite that they could lob at him from a safe distance; he didn't give himself much of a chance. If he could get close enough to them, and if he had time, he could blow everybody up, including himself, but that wasn't what he had in mind. At best, the four men would deny everything and proceed along as if they had important business elsewhere, and tomorrow night they would show up somewhere else, somewhere Jobim could not wait for them.

But the paddling stopped. Jobim heard the splash of an anchor and the rasping sound of the anchor line rubbing against wood.

They had stopped precisely where he had hoped they would—between five and ten yards down-tide from him, in the line of the drift. He heard something bang against one of the glass net-floats in the anchored boat, and a casual argument about the length of the fuse on one of the sticks of dynamite. He hoped the argument would turn bitter, even for a moment, for raised voices would cover any noise he might make.

Still lying flat on his raft, with his cheek pressed to the wood, he eased the red jug overboard and let it slip back in the tide. He could not place the jug yet—he would have to raise his head to do that—so he held the primer cord and waited for the men to busy themselves.

He heard the scrape of a match and saw the flaring light as it reflected off a stubbly chin. A hand cupped the match, and two fuses touched the flame. The fuses hissed briefly, then sparkled, and an arc of sparks flew off each side of the boat as the sticks of dynamite were thrown into the water. Immediately the men turned to the net and began carefully to prepare it for an orderly slide into the water.

Jobim raised up on his elbows and fed the primer cord behind his boat, letting it out a foot at a time, watching the white cord and hoping the men would not turn around and see it, trying all the while to see in his mind how far down the sticks of dynamite had fallen. It would be nice (not necessary, but nice) if the men could be made to believe that what had befallen them was the result of someone getting access to, and tampering with, their gear, for that would reinforce Jobim's scheme—to convince these people that they were known and marked. But for that, his explosion would have to be coordinated exactly with the detonation of the dynamite below.

He had the jug far enough back now, and he tied off the primer cord and picked up the squeeze generator and closed his eyes, envisioning the falling dynamite. His imaginary perspective was from the seamount, looking up, and he saw the two sticks falling in a slow spiral toward him, and almost on top of him, and so he squeezed the generator once, then again, then again, and he heard the wheel turn faster and faster as power built and built . . .

There was a sound of ripping as the primer cord detonated, and then as Jobim opened his eyes the world before him erupted. The water beneath the two boats bulged and burst, and in graceful slow motion the wooden boats disintegrated. The force of the explosion directly underneath them separated their planks and dispersed them, and as the bulge of water ruptured, it blew the four men upward, in disarray, like circus clowns on a trampoline.

In a microsecond before the unleashed energy reached Jobim's raft, he thought he had miscalculated and was going to follow the men into the air. But the rubber tubes lashed to his raft absorbed enough of the first hammer blow so that when the raft was heaved clear of the water it did not come apart, and it slapped back down on the sea in one piece, rocking crazily. Even his anchor held; all he had to do was keep from being rolled overboard. He reached into the plastic bag and brought out a powerful electric torch, one of those used to illuminate the surface of the sea for night fishing over the abyss. He did not turn it on, but knelt on his raft with the light in his lap, and waited.

There was new turmoil as the men hit the water and

sank and came up again and screamed, their shrieks tumbling over one another, unheard, for each man listened only to himself.

"Help!"

"I can't swim!"

"I'm hurt!"

"Oh, God!"

"Mother of Jesus!"

"I'm drowning!"

"Mother of God!"

"Help me!"

"Save me!"

"Jesus, Mary and Joseph!"

"Help help help!"

Eventually each man found a piece of debris to cling to, and their panic subsided and transformed into anger and outrage and bickering and worry about drowning and drifting away and being eaten by prehistoric monsters of the deep. Floating in the sea in daylight was bad enough; at night, it was the stuff of nightmares. These men were fishermen. They knew what kinds of things lurked down there, and they knew there were things they did not know, things that had bitten off steel leaderwire and straightened giant hooks, things that came up in the night to feed.

If only they could have the security of feeling their feet touch solid bottom . . . but out here, if their feet had touched anything, they would have gone into shock.

"What was that?"

"Nothing."

"Yes it was. I felt something."

"It's in your head."

"There it is again. Oh God!"

"What? What is it?"

"It's dead!"

"What's dead?"

"It's a fish! A dead fish!"

"Where? Where?"

"There's one! Oh God!"

"I felt one! It's all puffed up!"

"There's another one! They're everywhere!"

"Jesus!"

"I'm sick!"

"I told you that fuse was too short!"

"You fool!"

"Somebody must have . . . Oh God! Another one!"

"How far is it to . . . ?"

"Don't think about it."

"We're going to drown!"

"Stop it!"

"All of us! We're all going to die!"

"Shut up!"

"Holy Mary Mother of God . . ."

"Shut *up*!"

"I'm drifting away!"

"Kick this way, then!"

"I am, I am . . . Oh God! Guts!"

"Forget it!"

"There it is again!"

"What is?"

"It brushed me!"

Jobim switched on the torch, and the four floating men were stunned by the cone of light. They gasped and tried to look behind the light, but the beam was too strong, and they had to close their eyes or turn away. For a moment, they must have thought they were saved, for there were weak smiles. But when Jobim said nothing and did not move toward them, they knew they were not to be rescued, at least not now.

Jobim waited until he was sure their minds had passed through befuddlement and worry and into true fear, before he spoke. Then he spoke slowly and made his voice as low as he could, trying to sound like an oracle or a cave creature or, in any case, something mysterious and menacing that each of the men would recall in private moments and that would make them shiver and the hair rise on their arms.

"We are Los Vigilantes," Jobim said, and he paused for dramatic effect. "We have followed you and found you out, and we know you. You are evil men."

"No!" cried one. "We're just . . ."

"Quiet!" Jobim roared. He wished there were drums and thunder behind him. "You are evil men, and evil gets what evil gives. You would take the food from the mouths of babies and bring pestilence upon the land." (Words like that had to be effective, he thought. After all, that's the way they talk in the Bible.) "You will die."

"No!" the four voices howled in chorus.

"All men die. There is a time for dying, and your time will come. But perhaps not today."

Silence.

"Perhaps not tomorrow."

Silence.

"But be warned. Your faces are known to us now." He moved the light among the men, so the core of the cone, the brightest spot of light, shone briefly on each face. "One of us will always be with you, through all the days of your life. And when next you sin, know it will not be a secret sin, for the one of us who is with you will know." Jobim stopped. Something was taking shape in his mind, something mischievous. "You will not know who we are. We might be your closest friend, perhaps your brother. You can trust no one. No one. Never again.''

Slowly the circle of four men was growing wider, for they had not had the wit to hold hands and so were drifting apart. In a moment, Jobim would not be able to keep all four within the beam of light. "If ever you return to this place," he said quickly, "or to any other place to do the deed you have done, bid farewell to your loved ones, for you will not see them again."

Jobim switched off the light and sat still, hoping to appear to have vanished.

There were a few moments of silence. Then the men realized several things at once: They were not, after all, going to be rescued; if they were to survive, they would have to stay afloat until either they reached land or daylight came and a passing boat could pick them up; and, finally and most alarming, like ripples from a rock dropped into calm water, they were spreading farther and farther apart.

"Where are you?" called one.

"Here!" two answered at once.

"Come this way."

Splashes, swimming.

"Not that way! This way!"

"I did!"

"What's that?"

"Another dead fish. They're everywhere!"

"We're going to drown!"

"Shut up!"

"Shark!"

"Where?"

"I guess it wasn't."

"Jesus . . ."

Jobim sat on his raft and listened. The voices faded

quickly, for the tide was strong. They would be many miles away by morning, and probably miles from each other as well, for each man was an object of different density and buoyancy and resistance to water movement and would thus move at a different pace and be subject to different eddies and currents.

One or two might be picked up by boats, for there was occasional ferry traffic between the Mexican mainland and the Baja peninsula. They would be dropped at the ferry's next port of call and would have to work their way home, begging rides from village to village to island. And when they got home, what would they say had happened? Suppose one of their comrades had arrived before them. How would they coordinate their stories?

One or two were certain to drift onto uninhabited ground, there to scratch for survival until they could attract the attention of a fisherman going by or a family out to gather wood. There were lizards to eat if you could catch them, and a rattleless rattlesnake that tasted good if you could bite it before it bit you, and birds' eggs if you could find the nests hidden in the crevices in the high rocks. There wasn't much fresh water, and what there was lay in stagnant pools that probably contained bacteria that would make you sick. But you could survive.

Jobim doubted that any of them would die, and he did not consider himself responsible if one of them should die: He had cast them into the water whole and healthy and in good weather. Anyone should make it to shore who did not do something stupid.

Furthermore, if one or more of them did die, Jobim would have considered it justice, for in his opinion what they had done to the seamount branded them as no more worth preserving than a rabid bat.

Soon the voices were gone, and there were no sounds except the soft slapping of the water against the bottom of the wooden raft. Jobim pulled his anchor. As the killick came up and he reached for it, his weight shifted to one end of the raft, and that end dipped beneath the surface of the water. A big gold *cabrío* floated onto the raft, into Jobim's lap.

The concussion of the dynamite had not only killed the fish, it had disfigured it. Its belly was swollen; its tongue had inflated like a balloon and filled the yawning mouth; its eyes bulged from their sockets and stared in blank perplexity.

The seamount was dead now. It would be many, many months before life returned in any profusion, and years before it returned to anything like normal.

No, he would not be sad if one of the men did not make it all the way home.

XI

PALOMA WAITED FOR silence, and then waited some more, in case Jo had turned around and rowed back and was lurking nearby. At last she ducked her head underwater and came out beside the pirogue. She was alone on the sea.

She pulled herself up onto the overturned bottom of the pirogue and examined the hole Jo had dug with his harpoon. It was about the size of her fist, easy enough to patch with wood once ashore, but big enough to keep her from getting to shore.

She tried to think through her choices. She could stay with the overturned boat until she drifted onto land—tonight or tomorrow or the next day, or . . . It might be many days, and she might succumb to thirst or exposure. And suppose the weather went bad. To try to ride out a *chubasco* by straddling a hollow log was suicidal.

She could abandon the boat and swim for home. Absolutely, positively not. Not worth considering.

Or, she could try to patch the pirogue here and now.

With what? She had no wood, no canvas, no leather, no nails or tacks, no hammer. She could plug the hole with herself: She could sit on it. But then she couldn't paddle, because every time she moved the hole would open and water would rush in. She pictured everything she had brought with her, analyzing its potential to be shaped into a plug. Her hat? No, the straw fibers were too loosely woven; water would pour through them. Her flippers? She could cut one up and fit the piece of rubber into the hole. But the rubber wouldn't stay; it would float free. The glass faceplate of her mask? She had no way of securing it to the wood.

Her mind evaluated every item and discarded it. And then, as she looked at the wood fibers, she saw beside them other fibers, closely woven though not as thick as the wood, and she had the answer: her dress. She could stuff her dress into the hole, and it would keep the water out. The fabric was already saturated with salt water, so no more could penetrate it. And packed tightly in a ball, the cloth fibers would bind and become nearly waterproof.

She peeled the sodden shift up over her head, then ducked under the pirogue and, from the inside, packed the cloth into the hole. It made a tight plug—nothing that could survive a pounding in a heavy sea, but secure enough for an easy paddle on calm water.

She ducked out again, hauled herself up onto the bottom, and reached over and grabbed the far edge. Bracing herself on one knee, she pulled, and there was a liquid sucking sound and a pop as the suction broke and the pirogue jumped free of the water and righted itself. It was still full of water, though; only an inch of freeboard stuck above the surface. Since the boat was a hollow log, it would not sink, but if Paloma were to climb aboard, her weight would drive the pirogue's sides down flush with the surface. Every minuscule movement she made would tip the boat and allow more water to slosh aboard. She could not bail it out from inside.

So she clung to one side with one arm, and with the other hand began methodically to splash water overboard. She forced herself not to be impatient, for she knew that this was what she was going to be doing for the next several hours, probably well into the night. And she did not hurry, for she didn't want to tire herself and risk a cramp in an arm or leg. She could stop a cramp, but a muscle that had once gone into spasm was sure to cramp again unless it was rested for hours. Each succeeding cramp would be harder to relieve than the one before, and she did not want to be forced too early to use extreme remedies. It was said that the only way to relieve a terrible cramp was to cause worse pain elsewhere in your body, the theory being that the mind can only focus on one pain center at a time and it will concentrate on the most severe, and will thus stop sending cramp signals to the afflicted muscle.

Everyone, Paloma included, agreed that cramps could be affected dramatically by the mind. No matter what caused the cramp initially, you made it worse if you panicked, and you relieved it, to a greater or lesser degree, by detaching yourself from it and regarding it rationally as a muscle that has contracted and must be commanded to relax. Icy calm, of course, was a prescription more easily issued than filled, especially if you were swimming and the cramp knotted you up into a ball that reduced your buoyancy to a point where you could barely stay afloat, or if you were running, being chased by somebody or something, and a cramp knocked you to the ground.

As she continued to bail, the muscles in her upper arm

began to stiffen and ache. To be free to massage that arm with her other hand, she had to release her grip on the boat. Immediately the tide caught her and dragged her away from the pirogue, but she was confident of her strength as a swimmer and was not worried.

She was more than fifty yards away from the pirogue when she finally felt the fibers in her arm muscles relax and soften, and she stopped massaging the tissue. Unhurriedly, she began to breaststroke against the tide.

To anything observing her from below, she appeared to be a sizable, healthy animal going about its business, emitting no signs of vulnerability, no signals of prey. After ten or fifteen minutes, it had seemed she was not moving at all; she seemed no closer to her boat than when she had started.

But she had marked her beginning against a set of peculiarly shaped rocks on the bottom, and she knew she was making progress—very slowly, probably no more than a couple of feet with each stroke, and half of that she was losing before she could take her next stroke; but she was gaining ground. She was not tiring; she could swim like this indefinitely, and eventually—it might be a couple of hours from now—the tide would ease and she would gain a little more with each stroke. Then it would go slack, and she would gain still more. Finally it would turn, and she would make it to her boat in a few strokes.

Her left leg went first. She had a split-second warning, and then she felt her toes begin to roll over one another and snarl. She reached down with her hand and tried to squeeze the lower calf muscle, but it was too late. The muscle fibers had already balled into a knot the size of an orange. She rolled onto her back and used both hands to squeeze her leg. Kneading with her fingertips, she softened the knot and felt it begin to relax.

Suddenly the knot dissolved and she thought the cramp was finished and she straightened out her leg and then, before she knew what was happening, with a violent, almost audible spasm an even bigger knot lashed itself into the back of her thigh. Her heel snapped back against her buttock, like the blade of a jackknife closing.

She was drifting fast, was already much farther away from her boat. She told herself not to think about it, but to make an effort not to think about it was to think about it even harder.

She tried to use her hands to straighten out her leg, but her arms weren't long enough to give her adequate leverage. So she brought up her other foot and forced the toes between heel and buttock and pushed down.

Then the other leg went, a perfect mimic of the first one. And now she felt she was like one of the beggars on the carts in La Paz, the ones whose legs had been lopped off below the knee. She had no balance, she was top-heavy, and she rolled in the water like a trussed hog.

At first she thought she would faint from the pain. She *hoped* she would faint, for she was one of those people who tend to float on their backs, and as soon as she lost consciousness the cramps would disappear and she would roll onto her back with her head out of water.

When she didn't faint, she tried to swim toward her boat, using only her arms, but that was hopeless; she lost ground and grew quickly tired. She knew she had to attack the cramps with her mind.

So she stopped swimming and said to herself: You're drifting away. What is the worst thing that can happen? You'll drift so far that you can't get back to your boat on this tide. You won't drown because you know how to float forever (unless a *chubasco* comes along, and there's no use worrying about that now). So you'll drift

and drift, and sometime the tide will turn and take you
back toward your boat. Even if you drift wide of your
boat, all that will happen is that you'll travel until either
you strike land or someone picks you up. So, really, you
have nothing to worry about. (Somewhere, in the far
recesses of her mind, she knew she could not float
forever, or even for more than a few days. She would
fall victim to thirst or hunger or the sun. But her mind
did not let that knowledge intrude.)

Then she looked down through the water and saw
that there was one "worst thing" she had neglected. She
had drifted far off the seamount by now, and way
down, in the blue shadows just before darkness, were
two sharks, circling slowly. They were not the familiar
hammerheads. Even from this distance she could
discern the bullet shapes and the pointed snouts, and she
knew they were a kind of bull shark—quick, bold,
aggressive, ill-tempered, and completely unpredictable.

Each circle brought the sharks a bit closer to the surface; each circle was a bit quicker than the one before.
And Paloma knew immediately what was happening:
She was sending new signals, signals that said she was
no longer a sizable, healthy animal going about its
business—now she was a wounded, panicked animal
that could not defend itself and might make easy prey.

All right, she told herself: I've got to stop behaving
like this or they'll home in on me and tear me to pieces.
As she heard the words in her brain, she felt a rush of
panic, and so she tried even harder to straighten out her
legs; and the harder she tried the tighter they knotted.

What would it be like to be attacked by a big fish?
Would it hurt, or would it be so quick it wouldn't hurt
so much at all? No, it would probably hurt. What kind
of pain would it be? What's the worst pain you can
imagine?

She bit her tongue. Holy Mary, how that hurt. She bit harder. Nothing could hurt worse than this. She bit still harder, and now she tasted blood in her mouth and saw little puffs of red seep from between her lips into the water. The blood might draw the sharks closer.

But all she could focus on was the pain in her tongue. It was a blade, a flame, a needle.

The cramps collapsed.

She didn't know it until she stopped biting her tongue. As when you ease off on the throttle of an outboard motor, she expected the pain in her mouth to fade to a background, idle-speed sensation, and the pain in her legs to accelerate and take over. The pain in her mouth did fade, but nothing replaced it. She looked down and saw that her legs had unlocked themselves and the muscles in her calves were no longer twitching.

Very tentatively, she began to swim, aiming vaguely in the direction of her boat but more to test her muscles than to accomplish much. She used her arms and shoulders and let her legs follow along in a weak scissor-kick.

There was no pain, but there was no progress either. Her arms alone were not enough to move her body against the tide. Still, she kept swimming, to exercise the muscles and restore circulation to the tissue. She maintained a smooth and easy stroke, conveying calm and control.

After a few minutes, she looked down again, and she searched the edge of the gloom for the circling sharks. She saw only one and only part of that one, a flicker of gray shadow, heading away. She was a healthy animal once more, and to the sharks' perceptions a formidable foe instead of vulnerable prey.

She swam on for more than one hour, watching her boat grow smaller and smaller against the sea. Once in a while, a small muscle would give a warning twinge, a threat of spasm, and she would stop and massage the muscle and shake it. She did not want to stop for long, though, for continual exercise kept her warm, and warmth encouraged her blood to circulate. If she allowed herself to grow cold, her circulation would drop, her muscles would be starved for oxygen and they would cramp.

She swam without thinking, focusing on each stroke as an act of its own, independent of every other stroke and of all other acts, to be begun and completed with mechanical perfection toward an overall end that did not exist. She forced all other thoughts from her mind, for they could generate emotions that could alter her body chemistry and cause trouble—a cramp, a stitch in her side, a knot of gas in her stomach, or superhyperventilation, which could make her faint.

The first sign she had that the tide was changing was a feeling of warm, still water on her skin. She had swum into a mid-sea current that had slackened with the tide and was lying on the surface like curdled milk on a cup of coffee. She stopped swimming and looked around. The sea, which had been merely calm, was now flat and slick. Such swells as there were were so slow and lazy that she could not perceive them.

She saw a piece of floating weed and swam to it and threw it as hard as she could toward her faraway boat. It landed ten feet away and lay still. It didn't move to her, away from her, or off to one side. The tide was dead slack. Now if she swam she could not lose, she could only gain, and soon the new tide would begin and would push her along. Her pirogue was anchored, so it would not move.

With every stroke she took she imagined the boat growing infinitesimally larger. She traveled about a mile in the first hour, swimming on the slack tide. The second mile took her twenty minutes, for the tide had turned and begun to run. In another fifteen minutes she was sitting in her pirogue, working her fingertips into the soft tissue of her thighs.

She had been frightened, but now she felt proud, too, for she had survived on her own. Every decision had been hers alone to make, and every decision had been correct. True, Jobim had taught her the skills and given her the knowledge that helped her survive, but putting it all into practice, actually *doing* it, felt wonderful.

She shivered. The sun had dropped so far that the pirogue cast a sharp shadow on the sea. During the hours around midday, the sun had added heat to the water, and for a few hours more the water would retain that heat. But then the cooling air would leech the heat from the water. Paloma guessed that the temperature of the water had fallen five degrees or more since her boat had capsized.

Kneeling in the bottom of the boat, she scooped with her hands and splashed with her paddle, and scooped some more and splashed some more. She saw the sun slide to the horizon, then seem to hesitate, then plunge beneath it, leaving a sky of richer blue dotted in the east by faint stars. She saw a light or a campfire wink on a distant island. Nearby, somewhere behind her in the twilight, a small ray jumped into the air and slapped back down with a stinging splash, and Paloma started at the knowledge that out here she was never alone, day or night.

The boat was dry now, as dry as it would be until the sun could get at it tomorrow and evaporate the water from the wood. She had not been on the sea at night for a long time, so she double-checked the landmarks she could still see and stood up in the pirogue to search for the first lights of Santa Maria. Then she started to paddle toward home.

Miranda would be frantic. Paloma never stayed out this late, and her mother would *know* something had happened to her. She had drowned. Something had eaten her. She was injured and floating alone in the dark. Miranda's imagination would be working double time, and soon she would be resigned to the fact that Paloma was dead, that fate had torn another loved one from her bosom.

No, not fate. She would blame God, for it was God's will that Jobim should die, and now He had taken Paloma as well. Why? she would ask. Was He testing her? What did He want her to do? Why didn't He give her a sign? She would do anything, if only she knew what to do.

But God would keep Miranda from becoming hysterical in her grief. Once she had worked it out in her mind that Paloma's disappearance was divine will, there would be nothing she could do about it, including worry. After all, if God meant it to be, then to worry was implicitly to challenge God's will, to lament was to complain about God's will. Unthinkable.

Jo, of course, would be no help whatever. He would feign innocence and concern and would sympathize with Miranda's thought of the moment: If she was contemplating the mystery of God's will, he would shake his head in wonder. If she asked what she had done to deserve so cruel a fate, he would put an arm around her and assure her that hers was like the story of Job—she would be well rewarded in the Kingdom of Heaven. They would talk about Paloma and recall nice things about her and weep together.

The thought of the scene infuriated Paloma and made her paddle harder. But then she thought of the reception she would receive, after all this sentimental ritual, and she smiled. Miranda might even resent her return—very briefly—for she would have set her mind to martyrdom, and Paloma's arrival would be a second shock.

Jo would pretend to be delighted, but the pretense would be entirely for Miranda's benefit. He would skulk around, and in his eyes there would be a warning to Paloma to keep silent about what had happened today. Still, Paloma guessed that somewhere inside Jo there would be secret relief that she had returned, for she could not believe—despite his fits of rage—that his conscience could condone murder.

Probably Paloma would keep silent. For what would talking about today accomplish? There was no one to punish him, for even if people believed what she had to say, the offense would not seem serious. She had not been harmed. There was no way she could convey the recklessness, the willingness to hurt, that she had seen in her brother. He could not be punished for evil thoughts.

A three-quarter moon had risen in the black sky, and it cast a path of gold before the pirogue, a path that led Paloma home.

Her reception was almost exactly as she had imagined it: Miranda shrieked and clutched Paloma to her breast and thanked God for answering her prayers and proclaimed a miracle. She asked what had kept Paloma, and Paloma glanced at Jo and (unable to stop her tongue) said she had been foolish enough to let herself be delayed by nothing, really nothing, a stupid little tidal maelstrom that had carried her too far from shore. She should never have let it happen and (another glance at Jo) it wouldn't happen again.

Once more she had misjudged him. He didn't realize he was being teased. He viewed her explanation as another victory: He had warned her not to tell the truth, and she hadn't. He felt he was in control—of his mates, who had to respect him, if only for his daring; and of Paloma, who must fear him.

Jo crossed in front of Miranda and hugged Paloma— turning his head and touching her with the same affection with which he would have caressed a leper—and said he had been worried about her.

Miranda sensed something awry between her children. She could feel a current of hostility surging back and forth, and she knew that they were communicating in a kind of code that expressed nothing directly but sparked with hints of antagonism. She was apprehensive but helpless, so she covered her anxiety with a veneer of relief that everyone was home safe and sound.

And she was further diverted from worrying by the arrival of a few neighbors, who dropped in to chide Paloma for causing her mother concern and to tease Miranda about being so concerned. See? they said. We told you she'd be all right. Miranda interpreted that as a reprimand and responded to it by scolding Paloma for staying out so long. What she was really saying was: How could you cause me to make a fool of myself in front of my friends? Paloma knew that, and she apologized and said that yes, after all, she *had* been in some danger and was lucky to be back alive—thus justifying Miranda's concern and giving her a tale to tell her friends.

And through it all, Jo sat in the corner on a chair tilted back against the wall, and smiled.

XII

IN THE MORNING, Paloma did not go out to the sea-mount. She told Miranda that her terrible experience of the day before had frightened her and that she wanted to stay ashore for a day or two and help with the wash and the house. Miranda was pleased. Paloma could tell the other women in her own words what a miracle it was that she was still alive, so the other women couldn't accuse Miranda of exaggerating and they would see that her worries had been well founded.

Miranda also chose to regard Paloma's decision as a hopeful sign: Perhaps she was outgrowing this foolish-ness with the sea and would recognize and begin to accept a more traditional position in the community.

The reason Paloma stayed ashore was that she knew that if she went out to the seamount and watched Jo and his mates, she would not be able to keep silent, she would surely provoke another confrontation with them. And this time, someone would get hurt.

She had walked to the top of the hill above the dock and watched them and the other fishermen prepare their boats for the day. She could hear most of what was said and guess at the rest, for the conversation did not change much from day to day, and she knew that Jo was not telling the other fishermen where he and Indio and Manolo were going. Jo waited for the others to leave, pretending to be furious at being delayed by tangled fishing lines.

Paloma took some small comfort in his selfishness: If Jo was smart enough to know that it was against his interests to tell anyone about the new seamount, his greed would delay, for a while at least, the mass slaughter of the animals.

But she could take no comfort from the last piece of gear she saw Jo and Indio sling aboard: a big net, with lead weights at the bottom to drag the snare down to the top of the seamount.

When he was sure he was alone, Jo started his motor and headed to sea. He did not yet know precisely where the seamount was, but, given a whole day to search for it, with no pressure from Paloma or any competitors, he was certain to find it: With one of his mates peering through the viewing box, Jo would drive the motorboat in straight lines up and down the general area until, eventually, he would have to pass over the seamount.

Depending on the tide and the bottom currents and the movement of the vast schools of baitfish and of the other, tinier creatures at the small end of the food chain, it was possible that Jo might be prevented from doing much damage right away. He might toss his net and let it sink and haul in nothing but a stray pufferfish, for the big schools of robust jacks and *cabríos* moved constantly, following their own food, and catching them as they passed over the seamount was a random chance.

But it would happen—if not this morning, then this afternoon, if not today, then tomorrow—because with so many schools of so many fish passing over the seamount so many times every day, even if Jo's ignorance led him to anchor his boat in a wrong place at an inopportune time, he was bound, sometime, to spot a big school through the viewing box.

Paloma watched until the wake from Jo's motor melted into the moving water and the white hull of the boat itself was consumed by the shining light on the sea.

The dock was empty, so she could work on her boat without bothering anyone. She found some pieces of canvas and some pieces of plywood, and she cut and shaped them into patches that would block the hole inside and outside, and she nailed them in place and sealed them with daubs of pitch.

Then she walked back to the house.

Miranda was darting around the house like an agitated bird, and Paloma knew she was feeling a bit nervous, a bit excited, a bit apprehensive—a bit of a dozen different emotions, some of which complemented others, some of which contradicted others, and the sum of which confused her.

Mainly, Miranda was happy that Paloma would be staying with her and doing woman's work, and she wanted to make sure that the day was good for Paloma because she worried that if Paloma had a bad day she would go back to the sea, immediately and for good.

She longed to recover her daughter, to claim the companion Jobim had deprived her of by taking Paloma to sea. She wanted to be able to be proud of Paloma, proud of having a daughter who would be working with her. Raising a female child to do female work was a normal thing, a healthy thing, a good thing in the community. It made Miranda a normal person, someone to be accepted and treated like everybody else. She wanted to show Paloma off to the other women, partly as a symbol of her own achievement. But in the back of her mind she worried that Paloma might say or do something that would not seem normal, and that might make things more difficult than ever.

She was worried that the other women might not like Paloma and that Paloma might not like the other women. She wanted everybody to like everybody, but that meant that the women would have to contain their ceaseless complaining about everything. Paloma had been taught by her father that complaining was a waste of time. If something was not to your liking, went Jobim's guideline, change it. If it couldn't be changed, accept it. If you could neither change nor accept it, then alter your own circumstances to cope with it. But under no circumstances whine about it, because whining accomplished nothing but aggravation.

Paloma would have to be accommodating, too. She would have to conceal her contempt for complainers. And that, after all, was fair, because Paloma was not familiar with the women's lives and problems. She could not evaluate the genuineness or seriousness of the complaints.

If all you did all your life was wash clothes and clean house and cook food, why, then, the minute details of clothes-washing and housekeeping and cooking would be the most important things in your life. It was vital that Paloma be convinced that these details were not trivial and silly, at least not to the women, and so she must not scoff at them.

As Miranda flitted about the house, dusting things that didn't need to be dusted, cleaning things that were already clean, putting away things that she never put away, she started sentence after sentence, then stopped and started again, then tried another avenue of thought, then stammered and changed the subject. She was so fearful of being too specific that she was too vague, and it took Paloma several minutes to realize what Miranda couldn't say. When finally she caught on, she said, "Don't worry, Mama. We all have hands."

"What?" Miranda stopped.

"I row with the palms of my hands. They sew with their fingertips. If they cut one of their palms, it's nothing. They laugh at it. If I cut a palm, it's a tragedy. But if I cut a fingertip, it's nothing. We all have hands."

Miranda did not completely grasp why cut hands were central to the expression of what she had been trying to say, or to Paloma's comprehension of it, but there was an atmosphere of compassion to Paloma's voice that gave Miranda confidence that everything would be all right.

And it was, finally.

At first, the women treated Paloma carefully, eying her as a curiosity. This was only natural, since they had all regarded Jobim as a curiosity, and more—as an oddity, almost a menace. He had obeyed the laws and customs he agreed with and either rejected outright those he disagreed with (if he felt that they unwisely deprived a person of a freedom) or tolerated them with silent disdain (if he felt that they were harmless vehicles to convey the insecure along a path to self-regard). Jobim's attitude could make him appear superior, and he might have become intolerable to many people had he not shown just as piercing an eye for his own failings. Even so, there were men—mostly those who used rituals to give themselves stature they could not otherwise attain—who did not like Jobim and were not particularly sorry when he was no longer on the island. And some of those men were married to the women with whom Miranda worked. The women knew how close Paloma and Jobim had been and knew that Paloma had been behaving like her father's child. They would need to be convinced that Paloma intended to act more like a woman now.

She convinced them. She kept her mouth shut except to answer direct questions, and replied respectfully, even when she judged the questions to be either provocative or inane. She listened attentively to every monologue and nodded sympathetically, though the women's words made no impression on her brain: They rattled around like marbles in an empty shell, for the occupant of the shell was elsewhere—out on the water, imagining what was going on on the seamount.

She worked hard, abusing muscles she was not accustomed to using, never stopping to rest as most of the women did, not permitting herself a grunt of weariness or a sigh of tedium—until, that is, she discovered that the women wanted her to be exhausted and to appreciate physically the hardness of their lives. She did appreciate, and so she did echo a few of their complaints. And at the end of the day, several of the women took Miranda aside and complimented her on how well Paloma seemed to be turning out.

Walking up the hill under a heavy load of wash, Miranda was silent but obviously elated. Paloma thought that if the day had accomplished nothing else, it had given her mother some happiness, which was a rare and good thing.

Paloma did not stop wondering, though, how many animals had died during Miranda's brief happy time. She flayed herself for not stopping the animals from dying, even though she knew it was foolish of her to take the blame.

While she helped sweep the house and hang the wash

to dry and feed the chickens for the second time and stoke the cook fire, Paloma forced her thoughts to stay ashore. But as soon as the chores were done and Miranda turned to cooking the evening meal, Paloma went outside and looked at the sky to tell the time.

The sun was very low; it was late, later than Jo and the others would normally stay out. And as she looked toward the path that led down to the dock, she saw several of the fishermen strolling home, which meant that they had already been ashore for an hour or more, for it took that long to unload fish and clean them and swab the boat and stow the gear.

Perhaps some trouble had befallen Jo and his friends . . . nothing too serious, for Paloma was not capable of wishing real harm to anyone. But something inconvenient, time-consuming, uncomfortable, perhaps something frightening that might discourage them from returning again to the seamount.

Perhaps they had fouled their net on the bottom and had been capsized trying to retrieve it. They would have to right their boat and row home, for the saltwater-soaked motor would never start.

Or perhaps they had cast their net into a mass of king mackerel or wahoos and seen it torn to shreds as they struggled to free the thrashing, snapping animals before they could drag the boat underwater.

Perhaps now, as night approached, they were being harassed by a herd of porpoises who had smelled the fish in their boat and wanted some and were playfully bumping, jarring, slamming the boat with their noses and tails. The fishermen would toss a few fish over, and the porpoises would interpret that as encouragement to play even harder, so they would bump the boat from underneath on both sides and the boat would rock and spill more fish into the water, which would convince the porpoises that their game was a rollicking success and one to be continued with increased vigor. Jo and the others would hear the clicks and whistles and grunts as the porpoises chatted with one another, and in the thick, impenetrable blackness they would translate the conversations as the ravings of monsters. Soon they would panic and lose the balance of the boat and be tossed into the water, there to be engulfed in splashing, roiling foam filled with fish blood.

Paloma liked the last possibility best. Yes, that's what she could dream was happening to them if they weren't home soon.

But, walking toward the path to the dock, she suddenly realized there was a more likely reason for Jo's lateness—and it was a reason that made the palms of her hands go cold and wet, and then a trickle of sweat ran down her sides and a bubble of fear made bile rise in her throat.

From the top of the hill she saw that this was the true reason.

Jo's day had been successful beyond his dreams. They had netted so many fish and killed them and brought them aboard that they had had to drive the boat home at its slowest speed to keep it from swamping and sinking. The slightest wave of water would rush over the bow of the boat; the merest tipping of a railing would cause a flood.

As the boat puttered toward the dock, Paloma saw Jo and Indio and Manolo all sitting on fish, hip-deep in fish, surrounded by mounds of fish.

In a single day's netting they had caught more fish than in a month of line-fishing. But that alone was not what distressed Paloma. The great schools of jacks and *cabríos* could sustain—did sustain—heavy losses quite often, and they soon returned to full strength. There were so, so many of them, and they reproduced with such speed and in such profusion, and the sea was so vast that the few regular fishermen could not hope to catch up with them all; they could endure all but catastrophic onslaughts—dynamite, say, or a sudden invasion by the huge factory ships from the Orient, both of which were forbidden by law.

No. Worse for Paloma than the quantity of the catch was its quality, worse than the numbers were the species. Even from this distance and in the dwindling twilight she could see how Jo and his mates had fished, for they were pawing through the corpses in the boat and flinging overboard those that did not measure up to their suddenly high standards.

When they had caught little, they had taken everything and claimed to need every bit; they had to feed their families and sell the rest. There was no waste, they claimed, no disrespect. The death of anything gave life to something else. Very noble.

But now that they had plenty of fish—more than plenty—and the guarantee, as they saw it, of endless more, why should they bother to save anything that did not bring silver coins just as is, without further effort? Why bother with fish whose price was by the ton, not the pound, fish that had to be carted away and dried and ground up into meal? If those fish came up in the net and got killed, it was more economical to throw them away than to process them. And if some of them were fish that did *not* school, did *not* breed countless young so that many must naturally survive, did *not* exist in profusion on the seamount, well, to clean out these "trash fish" this way was probably efficient, probably a good idea, because it meant that each successive netting would yield a higher percentage of the more lucrative species.

As for maintaining a balance of life on the seamount, a balance that had taken nature scores of decades to establish, they would argue that it was well known how resilient nature was. Nature would always come back from anything. If this seamount was fished out, move on to another one, and by the time that one is fished out, maybe this one will be coming back. Or another one will. There is always more. You just have to be smart enough to find it.

By the time Jo and Indio and Manolo had finished culling through their catch, night had come, and they did the last of their work by the light of the rising moon. They were tired and hungry, so they did not bother to clean their boat or prepare their gear for tomorrow.

"We can do the boat in the morning," Jo said as they strode up the path. Paloma was crouching in the brush at the top, watching the three shadows approach.

"Now we know where the place is."

"And what's on it. Baby Jesus! I've never seen anything like that."

"I bet we could go late and be back by midday."

"We could go twice, do two trips a day."

"*You* go twice. One load like that's enough for me. My back's about to break."

"Maybe we ought to get another boat." This was Jo's voice, moving past Paloma and on up the hill.

"That'd mean more people."

"Why share?"

"We could double the catch."

"For the same profit, though. We'd have to go partners."

"No we wouldn't. We could make a deal: We take them there—maybe we blindfold them so they can't find the place again—then we take all our catch plus half of theirs."

"I don't know."

"Me neither."

"We meet after supper," Jo said. "To talk. We don't have to decide anything."

"Okay."

"Remember: Nobody talks to anybody. Or you're out." Jo added gravely, "Finished."

"Sure, sure."

The voices stopped and footsteps faded as the three dispersed, each to his home.

Paloma waited until she could hear no sound but the breeze rolling over the island. Then, staying in the shadow of the bushes in case someone should return for a forgotten tool, she crept down to the dock.

The moon was high enough so its light penetrated the shallow water by the shore and cast a faint mantle of white on the rocky bottom.

But there was little bottom to see, for most of it was littered with the dead.

There were floating corpses and corpses that had sunk, corpses that tried to bob to the surface but were blocked by others, corpses battered and mangled and without color, their brilliant capes faded into a sameness at death. And their eyes, all black and blank, stared glassily at nothing.

Jo and his mates must have thrown away a fourth of their catch, all but the biggest of the most valuable kinds, the ones that would bring at least a silver coin apiece. Here in the water by the dock were smaller jacks and yellowtails, a few little *cabríos*, and other groupers that should have been pulled from the net alive and put back in the sea immediately, for they were the future of their species.

Here too were those fish Jobim had called the innocents, those that had no market value, could not be sold as individuals, and were not worth gathering in the numbers, the tons, that would produce fish meal or cat food and be worth a few pennies at the factory.

They were the pufferfish, gentle and shy and gallant in their defiant instant obesity, contributors to no one's purse and no one's table, but hilarious jesters for anyone who dived into the sea.

They were the angelfish, whose chevrons changed color in every stage from infancy to adolescence to maturity, like an army man displaying seniority, radiantly beautiful at every age, the fluttering sentinels of the seamount.

The smaller rays—stingrays and leopard rays and eagle rays—recluses who hid beneath a veneer of sand and exploded in a puff at a stranger's approach, snared in flight from one hiding place to another.

A turtle so young, still soft of carapace, its wrinkled throat garotted by a strand of netting, its flippers limp, its tail a tiny comma flopping on the belly shell.

And others, like sergeant majors and parrot fish, grunts and chubs and hogfish and porgies, all killed and cast away to wash in the shallows and rot.

The carnage was immense; this was not fishing.

Here, kneeling on the dock, leaning over the edge and gazing into the water, Paloma saw her reflection shimmer in the moonlight, and she realized she was weeping.

She wanted to run up the hill and call out to the other fishermen, the grown men, and lead them down and show them this massacre, but she did not, because it was nighttime and her interruption would not be welcome. She wanted to bring Viejo down, and point out to his dim eyes all the bodies, all the waste. But she did not, because she knew her outrage would not be shared. There would be some tongue-clucking, some intentions expressed to teach the young men how better to cull their catches. But that was all.

And by morning, what she saw before her would be no more, for Jo was not an utter fool: They had arrived home at a full flood tide, and for the next six hours, as the tide ebbed, the bodies would be sucked out to deep water where some would sink and others would be eaten and others would be caught in passing currents and carried off somewhere, so that when the other fishermen arrived at the dock in the morning, all that would remain of the carnage would be a few floating fish and a few half-eaten skeletons on the bottom—a normal amount of flotsam and jetsam from a day's work.

Even now, the corpses on the surface were beginning slowly to drift away from the rocks on shore, obscuring her view of parts of the bottom but letting her see into new crannies.

She saw an animal between two rocks. It looked to be curled up, like a sleeping puppy, as if it had chosen to lie cozy in death. She dropped to her stomach on the dock and reached down and stretched for the bottom, wrapped her hand around slick and solid flesh and brought it up and set it on the dock.

It was a green moray eel, young and unscarred, and more than any other of the animals it touched her. For while the other animals were simply dead, not alive anymore, this moray was contorted in the agony of its death, frozen at its final moment. It was tied in a knot that made it seem to be more than merely dead: It seemed that it would be dying forever.

This was a hideous snapshot of an animal that in life had had dignity but that in death had been transformed into a gargoyle.

Paloma knew well that morays often died in this

grotesque way. It was, in one strange sense, a natural death, for it reflected the morays' behavior in life.

Morays lived in holes or small caves or crevices or under rocks, and they lurked at the entrance to their lair, mouth open, gills pulsating rhythmically, hypnotically, skin color blending with their surroundings.

When prey passed by, the moray would shoot out its body—a single tube of muscle—and snatch the prey and begin to swallow it. The mean-looking fangs in the mouth were but gatekeepers: Beyond, back in the throat, was another set of teeth that gripped the prey and forced it down, down in rippling spasms, down into the gullet.

If the prey was large, larger than the eel's weak eyesight had anticipated, and if it struggled and threatened to yank the eel from its hole, the eel would anchor its tail around a rock or a coral boulder and contract its central muscles until no free-swimming prey could resist.

Thus, breath-hold divers were doubly careful about poking around in holes in reefs. First, there was the fear of being bitten, because the bite was excruciating and the wound it caused was ragged and would not close and the eel's mouth was coated in a slime that contained virulent infectants. But worse than the bite was the knowledge that if the eel grabbed a hand or a foot or a shoulder and could not sense the size of the prey (for it would not actually try to eat something so much bigger than itself as a human), it would anchor its tail and sink its fangs deeper and hold on until the prey stopped thrashing and the eel could come out of its lair and see what it had caught.

Once in a while, a moray would catch itself unawares —half out of its hole or swimming in the ocean from niche to niche—would snatch a prey and have no rock on which to fasten a grip. Then it would tug against itself.

It would whip into a perfect knot, wrapping the tail around the head and back down through the loop made by neck and body, and it would pull its prey through the loop, flopping and bouncing and rolling down the reef and out into open water—secure that it had an anchor and its prey did not.

Mostly, the eels knotted themselves this way when they encountered a force stronger than they—like a steel-barbed hook that fastened in the back of their throat and was attached to a filament that slid between the fangs and could not be bitten off and was connected, finally, to a man on a boat above who had strength and patience and the ability to tie off his line and let the moray exhaust itself.

Fishermen hated morays. They bit at any bait, large or small, so there was no way to avoid catching them. They were useless, for no customers would buy them and no islanders would eat them. They were dangerous: They were never dead by the time they reached the boat, and they were always tied in a slimy, slippery knot, and unless you were prepared to cut away and lose your leader and swivels and hook, you had to retrieve the hook from down deep around the second set of teeth in the throat. The boat was rocking, the eel was thrashing, the other fishermen were grousing because you were upsetting them and their gear and the boat itself, while you tried to bash the eel on the head and render it unconscious so you could slit its gills or get inside its mouth with a pair of pliers.

The combination was perfect for a severe, painful, perhaps incapacitating bite.

So moray eels were "bad" animals—ugly, useless, dangerous, probably offspring of the devil or, at least of some of his underlings.

One day, Jobim had hooked a moray and brought it up to the boat. It was tied in a knot, and as it struggled in the water it swung like the pendulum of a clock. Paloma had never seen a live moray before, and, looking down through the roiled water, she did not know what it was. It looked like a mess of living weed.

"Give me the pliers," Jobim had said.

She handed him the pliers and watched as he gently brought the eel to the surface.

"Hold this." He had passed her the fishing line, and she felt it twitch and thrum with the eel's desperation. He held the pliers in his right hand and, with the same hand, slid two fingers down the leader to within an inch of the eel's mouth. Then he pinched the leader and pulled the eel clear of the water and, with his left hand, grabbed the eel behind the head and squeezed.

She had never imagined a creature like this. It wasn't a fish, it was a monster. Its black pig's eyes bulged and glistened. Its mouth was agape and strung with strands of mucous slime. Its gills, what she could see of them amid the pile of bulbous green flesh, throbbed. It grunted. It hissed.

"Kill it!" she shrieked. "Kill it!"

"Why?"

"Kill it!"

"You want it dead, you kill it." Jobim had nodded at the cudgel he kept in the boat to stun sharks.

"Don't *you* want it dead?"

Jobim didn't answer. He was staring fixedly into one of the eel's eyes. The muscles in his arms and shoulders flexed and twisted as he fought to keep the eel from writhing free. Then he squeezed harder with his left hand, and the eel's mouth opened wider, and he squeezed still harder, and the two jaws separated and made a line that was almost vertical, as if the bottom jaw had unhinged completely.

Jobim opened the pliers and pushed his hand into the eel's mouth.

"He'll bite off your hand!" Paloma had cried, and she grabbed the cudgel and raised it with both fists over the eel's yawning mouth.

Jobim pushed his hand farther down the gullet, and Paloma saw the eel's flesh bulge as his knuckles passed through. His hand was gone, and his wrist, and half his forearm. Still the eel writhed and hissed, and every fiber in Jobim's left arm danced. He lowered his eyes closer to the eel's eye, and he probed with the pliers, feeling for the barb of the hook. He found it, and his hand twisted beneath the pulsing green skin, and slowly his arm and wrist began to withdraw, coating with shiny slime, and his hand came free, then the pliers and the steel hook.

Still holding the eel's head in his left hand, he lowered the entire body back into the water and slowly sloshed it back and forth to get water flowing once again over the gills. When he was sure the eel would not succumb to shock and stop breathing, he released it.

The ball of green muscle sank a foot or two, then uncoiled like a waking snake, then wriggled to stretch the tired tissues, and then—suddenly aware and awake and sensing that it was vulnerable in open water—it darted with quick, snapping thrusts toward the bottom.

Several times Paloma had asked Jobim why he hadn't killed the moray, and, annoyingly, he had persisted in answering her question with a question. He was busy untangling the fishing line that had coiled around his knees as he fought to free the moray.

"Why should I kill it?"

"It could've bitten your hand off."

"It could not have bitten my hand off. It could have bitten me."

"Isn't that bad enough?"

"To make me kill it? No. I hooked the animal by accident. I hurt it. I put a hook in its throat and dragged it out of water, where it knew it couldn't breathe and was going to die—instinct told it that—and I squeezed its head so hard that its mouth had to open, and then I jammed a steel thing and a big bone down its throat and poked around and caused it pain and terror. Bitten me? I wouldn't have blamed it for biting my head off. Now, why, on top of all the things I'd already done to that animal, should I kill it?"

As Paloma opened her mouth to speak, Jobim added quickly, "And don't say, 'Why not?' 'Why not kill?' is a question you must never ask. The question must always be 'Why kill?' and the answer must be something for which there is no other answer."

Paloma had no good answer for "Why kill?" and so she said nothing.

That afternoon, when they had finished fishing, Jobim had moved the boat to the shallowest part of the seamount and told Paloma that he would take her for a dive. She was tired and didn't feel much like getting wet, but a dive with Jobim always promised fun and excitement and was a treat she would never decline.

Jobim cut a fish into small pieces and put them in a plastic bag tied to his waist, and together they pulled themselves down the anchor line. On the bottom, he motioned for her to stay at the anchor line, and he went off among the rocks, looking for something. Soon he had found whatever it was, and he waved her over to him. His face was six inches from a crevice in the rocks, and he pulled her down beside him.

In the second that it took her eyes to focus and her mind to recognize what she was gazing at, she concluded that her father had gone mad and was trying to kill her.

Guarding the crevice with its gigantic head and puffing cheeks and black eyes and gaping mouth was a moray eel so large that it made the other one seem like a garden snake. Its head filled the hole, and each time the gills rippled they scraped the coral sides. Paloma believed that if the eel should shrug, it could consume her entire skull.

She jerked backward in reflex, but Jobim caught her arm and forced her to return to his side. He took a hunk of fish from the bag at his waist and held it up to the moray's face. For a moment the eel did not move. Then it slid slightly forward, as if on a mechanical track, and Jobim dropped the morsel of fish; the eel let it fall into its mouth and closed its mouth and swallowed, and the gills rippled in unison and the eel slid backward into its hole.

Jobim fed it another piece, and another, and by then he knew that Paloma was short of oxygen so he motioned that they would go up.

As they rose, Paloma looked down and saw that the eel had slid more of its body—four or five feet—out of the hole and had turned its head and was looking up at them. Then it must have decided that they were truly gone, for it slid back and disappeared.

When, on the surface, Paloma tried to speak, Jobim waved her silent and touched his chest, signaling that he wanted to hurry and return to the bottom.

This time the eel seemed to have watched the last part of their descent, for its head was a foot outside the crevice and its eyes were tracking them.

Jobim handed Paloma the bag of bait. She shook her head, no: She wouldn't do it. But he forced the bag into her fist and put a hand on her shoulder in assurance and embrace.

She knew enough to keep the bag itself concealed, for any fish, once it knew the location of the source of the morsels you were feeding it, would ignore individual bits and would dive for the bag and rip it away from you.

The first piece she held a full two feet from the eel's mouth, until Jobim pushed her hand closer. The eel slid forward; Paloma dropped the bit of fish; the eel swallowed.

With each new piece she grew bolder, for the eel made no motion to do anything but what she intended, and the last piece from the bag she actually lay within the eel's lower jaw and pulled her hand back well in time for it to close its mouth on nothing but the fish.

Back on the surface again, she was elated and amazed. Her thoughts came so fast that her words could not keep up with them. Finally, by pointing and puffing and speaking as slowly as she could, she was able to convey to Jobim that she wanted to cut up another fish and return immediately to feed the moray.

"Not me," he said somberly. "He could bite my hand off."

"What?"

"It's too dangerous."

"But . . ."

"I think we should kill him before he hurts somebody."

Now Paloma knew what Jobim was doing, and she screamed and splashed water at him, and he threw back his head and laughed.

While they rested, he cut up a bigger fish into bigger pieces, for the moray had been bigger than he had guessed it would be. He told Paloma that morays were like sharks, in that you never knew how big an individual might be: The hole you poked your hand into might contain an eel no longer than your arm and not as thick, or it might house a creature taller than a man and as broad as his chest. This one was probably seven or eight feet long, and its head was more than a foot wide.

They had spent many minutes away from the eel, and it was not there when they returned. But as soon as one of their shadows crossed before the crevice in the rocks, the huge green head slid forward and hung there, gills and mouth pulsing together.

Jobim was like a dog trainer, teaching the animal to beg for its food. Each morsel he held farther and farther from the hole, urging the eel to slide farther out. But he did not tease the animal: When Jobim had established where the food would be, there he left it. The eel's decision-making machinery was rudimentary and primitive, and if Jobim had pulled the food back after the eel had committed to exposing itself a certain distance, the eel might have registered signals of betrayal and danger, which might have driven it into a defensive posture, which might have expressed itself in an attack on Jobim.

The eel would not come all the way out of the hole. Apparently, it needed the security of knowing that its tail was anchored in the rocks so that if anything should go awry, it could dominate the encounter.

And as Jobim told Paloma when they were back in the boat, he saw no reason to encourage the animal beyond its own limits, especially on first meeting.

"You mean we can do it again?" It hadn't occurred to her that something so special could be repeated.

"We'll see. Some people can."

"What do you mean?"

"With most people, something like that is luck. They get there, the conditions are right, the animal doesn't feel threatened, he's hungry, they don't do anything stupid, so they succeed. But they—the people—are not in control. They're just fortunate that things went their way. Some people, very few, *make* it happen. There's something—I don't know what it is, maybe it's like the sounds we can't hear and the sights we can't see. Some people have something special with animals. It may be the same thing some animals have with each other, that they send and receive each other's signals so they understand each other. By nature, animals in the wild don't trust people, and they shouldn't. But these few people, the people who have this thing, animals trust."

"You have it, then."

"I have a little of the good thing, but not a lot. I never know from animal to animal. Maybe we were lucky with this eel today. Maybe he was in a good mood. We'll see."

Paloma said hopefully, "Maybe I have a lot of the good thing."

"Maybe. But don't hope too much. It's nice, the good thing, but it can be dangerous, too."

"Why?"

"You can believe in it too much, believe you can do anything. You try to put yourself in the animal's mind and imagine yourself as the animal, and suddenly you think you can control it. You forget that you're a human being and *it* isn't. You try to reason with it. It can't reason. You take one step too many. If you're lucky, you end up with scars and a good lesson. If you're unlucky, you get hurt. Or killed."

They had returned to the eel the next day after fishing. As Jobim set the anchor, Paloma had asked if he thought the eel would still be there.

"Why would it go away? Where would it go?"

"How would I know?"

"Animals usually have a reason for going somewhere or staying somewhere. *They* don't know they have a reason, but their bodies know. Their instincts tell them. Most sharks have to move because if they don't they'll sink to the bottom and drown. Simple. Schools of fish have to move because the little things they feed on move, and if they're to continue to eat they'd better keep up with their food. Reef fish stake out a territory on the reef and patrol it all their lives unless something comes along and drives them off. Moray eels will find a hole and make it their own as long as enough food passes by for them to grab. When it doesn't, they'll find another hole. This big fellow has no reason to move now: He has comfort, safety and, best of all, since yesterday he doesn't even have to hunt. Some fools are bringing him dinner."

The eel was there, hovering in its hole, and it had to be coaxed to take the first bite of fish.

He's sulking, Paloma thought. He's angry because we went away.

Once the feeding reflex was stimulated, the eel became ravenous. More and more of it hung out of the hole, and Paloma, her confidence blooming, backed farther away, trying to bring the eel entirely out into the open.

She did not see, and never knew, that Jobim, as he stood a foot or two to one side, had a knife clenched in the fist he held behind his back.

She fed the eel five separate pieces of fish as it hung in the water, stabilized by barely perceptible ripples of the fins that ran along the top and bottom of its body.

There were half a dozen pieces of fish left in the bag,

and now Paloma took a piece of fish from the bag with her left hand and slowly, calmly drew it wide and back toward her shoulder. With a brief shudder, the eel followed the fish.

Paloma drew it back around her head, where she slipped it into her right hand and continued to lure the eel around behind her. The eel's tail was over her left shoulder, its head over her right, when she gave it the piece of fish. It swallowed the fish and stayed there, wrapped around her shoulders like a fine lady's stole.

She fed it two more pieces of fish, and there were three left. She glanced at Jobim and saw that his eyes were wide and the veins on either side of his throat were thick as anchor line. For a second she thought he was afraid for her, and perhaps he was, but then it struck her that neither of them was breathing, could breathe, and yet both had to breathe.

Paloma took the last pieces of fish in her right hand, squeezed them into a ball and held them up before the eel's open mouth. She pushed them upward so the eel would have to rise slightly to reach them, and as it did she ducked down and pushed backward with her feet and shot on a sharp angle toward the surface.

Jobim didn't chastise her; he didn't have to. Each knew what the other was thinking, and mostly their thoughts were the same: Paloma had been reckless but had succeeded, had taken a risk and had won; she had the good thing, probably a lot of it, but it was something she would have to learn how to use. And she should not try stunts like this without Jobim close by.

All the way home in the boat, they had only one exchange:

She had said, "I think I'll call him Pancho."

He had replied, "It's not a 'him.' It's an 'it.' It doesn't have a name, and don't give it one."

Still, she had permitted herself to think secretly of the eel as Pancho, and every day she was out with Jobim she had looked forward at the end of the day to visiting with Pancho.

On every visit the eel would curl around her shoulders, sometimes after only a bite or two of fish. Occasionally, it would let its weight drop onto her shoulders, and it would lie there, and she could stroke its smooth skin while she fed it.

And then one day it was gone.

Paloma thought they had come to the wrong hole, but the landmarks underwater were too familiar. They searched every hole in that section of the seamount, then swam over the rest of the seamount, hoping that if they passed close enough to the eel's new hole, it would come out. But it had gone.

"You said it wouldn't go away." Paloma felt hurt, deceived, as if either Jobim or the eel had tricked her into believing that if she fed the eel, it would stay there, for her, forever.

"No I didn't. I said it would have to have a reason to move. I guess a reason came along."

"What reason?" No matter what her father said, she would challenge it. She wanted to prove him wrong, to show him up, to make him feel guilty by being . . . by being what? She didn't care. She wanted to punish him for her disappointment.

"I don't know. Maybe a secret clock inside him said it was time to go somewhere else. Maybe a secret calendar said it was time to find a mate."

"I thought you said he wasn't a 'him.' You said he was an 'it.'"

Jobim smiled, and, seeing him smile, Paloma could not resist smiling, too.

"*It*, then. Maybe it got foolish and tried to eat

something too big, and that something turned around and ate it.''

"What could eat it?''

"Only a big shark. No, I don't think that happened. He might have gotten old and gone wherever eels go to die.''

"Do they go somewhere to die?''

"I don't know. That's what I mean: We don't know. We *can't* know. He was here yesterday and he isn't here today. There's nothing we can do about it.''

"But . . . he liked us. I could tell.''

"Don't do that to yourself, Paloma.'' Jobim had stopped smiling.

"He knew us. I know that.''

"We accustomed it to us as feeders. That's all. It didn't *like* us. It won't *miss* us. It doesn't have feelings like that. It isn't that level of being.''

"How do you know?''

"I . . .'' Jobim stopped, and looked at Paloma, and smiled again. "I don't, not for sure.''

"What about the good thing?''

"You have the good thing, as much as anyone can have it with an eel. With anyone else, it would have stayed in its hole or taken a bite out of them. It trusted you. That's what the good thing is, trust.''

Now Paloma knelt on the dock in the moonlight and held the knotted eel in her lap. Gently, she tried to undo the knot, to reduce the hideousness of the slaughter, to erase the reminder of the eel's last agony. She pushed the slippery tail up through the loop made by the coiled body, then pulled it through the loop and lay the body on the dock. But rigor mortis had already gripped the animal, and the flesh was set in a gnarled contortion. It would not straighten out, but rocked on the wooden dock and banged its rigid snout against the planks.

She picked up the eel and dropped it off the dock. It fell on top of other corpses that were slowly being swept toward deeper water, and then it sank beneath them.

Still kneeling on the dock, Paloma let her glance travel along the path of gold cast on the water by the moon. It did not begin or end, but seemed simply to happen, magically, somewhere out there in the blackness this side of the horizon, and to disperse, spent, somewhere in the blackness behind her.

If ever she thought of trying to place her father, to locate him where he was now (and she avoided doing this often, for her mind could not cope with it and it made her uncomfortable and stretched her belief so far it seemed it must break), she located him there, between the sky and the sea, at the source of the path of the moon.

"What can I do?" she said aloud, to Jobim. "Don't say Nothing, because that's what I've been doing, and look what's happened." Paloma gestured at the water. She didn't wait for a response she knew would never come. "They're going to kill our seamount, and when they've killed ours they'll move on to another one and kill that, too, and they'll get richer and richer, and because they're blind, they won't see where it has to end. And I can't do anything about it because I'm alone and nobody will listen to me and even if they did they wouldn't do anything. Mama doesn't know anything about it, and if she did, she'd say it was God's will and that's that." Paloma paused, fearing she had given offense. "I'm sorry, but that's the truth and you know it. Viejo says anyone can do anything he wants, and if all the fish are gone one day, well, that's the way of the world."

Now she shouted into the night. "But it's *not!* I won't let it be!" Her words echoed across the water.

"All right. I'll be calm. But we can't just let it happen. It's yours, too, you know, not just mine. It's everybody's. I'll do what I can, but I don't know what to do! I can't go blow them up, like you did. I couldn't kill them. I couldn't."

She was gazing at the spot where the gold seemed to begin. She did not expect a response, and she did not receive one, not in the sense of an answer: No words rang in her head, no solution sprang into her breast. Nor was she "visited," the way people said they felt when they had a religious experience, where an angel touches your life and changes you. And certainly she did not sense the presence of a deity. There were no thunderclaps or great winds or deep voices.

But something did begin to happen inside her.

It was a warmth that started at her fingertips and seemed to creep up her arms and over her shoulders and down into her chest and through her stomach and into her legs. For a second she recognized it as the same kind of sensation she had when she was about to faint, but there was no faintness, no lightheadedness at all. It was, rather, a fullness, as if something missing had finally been put into place.

And that missing something, now that it had been found, seemed to impart an order to things, for she felt a purpose and a sense of confidence and a sure knowledge that there was an answer and that she would find it if she obeyed her natural instincts instead of bending to the whipsawing of conflicting emotions and impulses.

What those instincts would tell her to do and what the answer would be and what any of it would mean for her or for the seamount or for anything, she had no idea.

But so suffused was she with this feeling, and so

positive was she that it meant *some*thing, that once again she gazed at the spot in the sky where the gold began, and she nodded.

Supper was over by the time Paloma returned to the house, and the plate of food Miranda had left for her on the table was cold, but the new feeling that was running through her was consuming energy, so she was hungry and she sat down to eat.

Jo was there. Normally by now he would have been in his room, but he had lingered.

"Did you have a good day?" he asked Paloma.

Paloma's mouth was full, and she did not respond right away.

Jo said, "I had a *fine* day."

Miranda said, "That's nice," to cover the fact that Paloma had not replied. She was determined that there would be civility in the house, even if she had to fabricate and maintain it herself.

"Many more days like this, I'll have enough money for school."

"So," Miranda said, "you will leave me, too."

"Too? Papa didn't leave you."

"No? Where is he, then?"

"He didn't go away on purpose."

"If he had lived a normal life," Miranda said, and Paloma was surprised at the bitterness in her voice, "like a normal person, he would be here today." She looked at Paloma, her eyes urging her to learn the lesson.

"We don't know that," said Jo. "But that's what I want to do—live a normal life."

"In some stinking garage in Mexico City?"

Jo ignored his mother's remark and said to Paloma,

"I think Papa would have wanted it for me, too, don't you?"

Paloma looked at him but said nothing.

"Sometimes I think that's why I found the seamount. I think maybe he led me there." Jo smiled. "Don't you?"

Paloma clenched her teeth and kept silent.

Jo spoke this time to Miranda. "This seamount of Papa's is very rich. By the time I'm through with it, it will give me enough money to take care of all of us. You won't have to worry about money again, Mama." His eyes shifted to Paloma. "Viego always says that the sea exists to serve men, and I know Papa would agree. Yes, this seamount is what he left us, and I will see that his will is carried out."

Now it took all Paloma's strength to keep her mouth shut. It outraged her that Jo was summoning their father's spirit to justify ravaging the seamount. But she knew Jo was trying to enrage her, to goad her into a discussion in which she had to be the loser: If she agreed with him, she would be sanctioning the destruction of the seamount in Jobim's name; if she disagreed, she would appear selfish, short-sighted, and unconcerned with Miranda's welfare.

So she busied herself with her food until Jo had yawned and stretched and left the house to go to his room.

Preparing for bed, Paloma knew that Miranda was looking at her and was worried. Miranda had felt the mute fury in Paloma's silence, and had taken more alarm in Paloma's lack of response than she would have in a fiery argument.

Miranda sensed that something was afoot, and she was right. She didn't know what, of course. But then, neither did Paloma.

XIII

PALOMA STOOD ON the hill and watched Jo and his mates prepare their boat for sea. Again they waited for the others to depart, for they were determined—especially now that they knew how rich the seamount was—to keep its location their secret.

Paloma guessed that the evening before they had been questioned by other fishermen about their formidable catch, and they must have mumbled or evaded or lied outright, for today they started out in the wrong direction and changed course toward the seamount only when they were confident they were being neither followed nor observed.

Paloma returned to the house and puttered around for a while. She was not upset about accomplishing nothing, for she had no intention of doing anything specific. She had no plan. She did not know why she had returned to the house, though it seemed as good a thing to do as any other.

She was coasting, riding the day, letting it take her

where it would, and she felt as if she were outside herself looking in, watching with a detached interest. It was not that she felt guided by something or someone else, it was more an inner assurance—based on nothing rational at all—that whatever was going to happen would happen.

Miranda eyed Paloma nervously from time to time but made no comment. She suggested things for them to do—move this bed and sweep under it, take that mat outside and beat the dust out of it—and Paloma agreed instantly and worked diligently. But Paloma was not really there.

At midday, Paloma said she was going for a walk, and Miranda nodded. As far as Paloma knew, she *was* going for a walk; she had no fixed destination. But once she neared the top of the hill that led down to the dock, the sea summoned her so powerfully that she could not possibly resist.

She went to the dock and pulled her boat out from beneath it and noted that her fins, marks, snorkel, and knife were in the pirogue and that her patch had sealed the hole in the bottom. She climbed aboard and paddled toward the seamount.

Their backs were to her as she approached. They were setting their net, letting it catch the tide and billow and sink in a wide, deep arc. When it had settled, they would pull an end of the net into each end of the boat, tightening the purse, forcing the mass of fish into a ball of panic. Their boat sat high in the water, which meant that so far they had made no good casts or, perhaps, had not yet tried, waiting instead for the big schools to come by. This cast alone, if it were good, could fill their boat.

They would go home richer but unsatisfied, knowing that if one cast could produce a catch worth so much money, two or three could double or treble their reward.

So tomorrow they would probably tow a second boat, maybe a second and a third. Their secret would be harder and harder to keep, and soon the entire fleet would be there.

They did not see her or hear her, and she knelt in the pirogue up-tide, adjusting her position with little flicks of her paddle, watching. If they had turned around and asked what she was doing, she would not have had an answer. She was there; that was all she knew.

After a while, Indio did chance to turn and he nudged Jo, whose head snapped around, eyes narrowed.

They eyed each other for a long moment, until Jo turned back to his net and said casually, over his shoulder, "Come to watch?"

She did not respond, but stayed where she was, a dozen or so yards from their boat, looking at their backs. Jo made sure he was elaborately occupied with the net, but his mates were obviously distracted and unsettled by her presence. As they paid out the net, they muttered to one another, and though Paloma could not discern who was saying what, she grasped the sense of the conversation.

"What does she want?"

"You think she'll do anything?"

"Like what?"

"She wouldn't dare."

"She better not."

"I don't like it."

"Shut up."

"What about the net? We said . . ."

"Forget it. She's beaten. She's given up."

"Then what's . . . ?"

"Forget it, I said. Watch this." Jo scooped a handful of rancid fish guts from the pool of oily water at the stern of the boat below the motor and cocked his arm and flung the mess toward Paloma. It fell several feet short of the pirogue. Instantly, a pack of sergeant majors materialized and devoured it.

Paloma did nothing, said nothing, in no way acknowledged the gesture.

"See?" Jo said to the others. "She won't do anything. We've talked. She knows what's what. Now: Look through the glass and tell me if they're still there."

Manolo put the viewing box on the surface of the sea and looked down. "Right there. They haven't moved. God! Look at them all! We won't get 'em all in this boat."

"Then we'll tow 'em home in the net. Tomorrow we better bring a barge out here. This is too good."

Though Jo did not look at Paloma as he spoke, she knew he was speaking for her ears, taunting her.

But still she said and did nothing, for she didn't know what she could say, or what she could do. If her silence annoyed any of them, that was fine; speaking could only strip away the mystery about why she was there. Perhaps if they became genuinely angry they would make a mistake and lose their net or stagger clumsily and capsize their boat . . . But these were fantasies, idle wishes, hopeless hopes.

Their net was cast and was sinking, and they were concentrating on each foot of fiber to make sure it didn't foul against anything or snarl itself into a tangle. When it was all the way out, they would let it sit for a few minutes before hauling it in—to give ample time for masses of fish to wander into the trap.

Paloma felt a faint touch of pressure on her knees, a slight surge that lifted her pirogue an inch, no more, and let it settle again. It might have been the wake of a distant boat, but there were no boats in the distance; it might have been the wave from a breaching animal, but no animal had breached hereby; it might have been the weakening signature of a long-distance seismic wave, but that she would see travel on the surface and lift Jo's boat, too.

Only her boat had moved, which meant that whatever was happening to cause the change in the water pressure was happening directly beneath her.

She cocked her head over the side of the pirogue and backpaddled so she would have a better angle on the water below. All the water looked black, which didn't strike her as peculiar until she realized that the water farther away was its normal blue.

Then she knew immediately what had fooled her eyes, and she smiled to herself. The manta had returned. It was lying a few feet below the surface, and the black carpet of its back was so close that it seemed to extend to the horizon.

Then, silently, she reprimanded herself, for there was no reason to believe it was the same manta ray. There were many manta rays around seamounts, and she had chanced to paddle her boat into the vicinity where one was cruising, and it had probably noticed the shadow her pirogue had cast and had moved over to take cool shelter in it. Rays that came to the surface in the heat of the day often took refuge beneath a ship or a dock, for direct sunlight quickly became uncomfortable. It was a simple, instinctive, animal thing to do, and for Paloma to attribute more or different sensibilities to so primitive an animal she knew to be folly.

But she wanted to be positive nonetheless, so she pitched her anchor overboard and let the line pay free from the pirogue, then held her mask to her face and bent over and put the faceplate on the water.

It could not be the same manta. There was no wound, no sore, no shredded flesh. Yet there was *some*thing

strange about the area around the left horn. It looked
dented or nicked, as if there had been an injury some
time ago. Could there be two enormous mantas on the
same seamount with an injury in the same place? She
could not believe it possible, so she decided to go down
and look.

The fishermen still had their backs to her, were still
setting their net, so they did not notice when Paloma
slipped over the side and took a few deep breaths and
disappeared.

When the net was set a moment later, however, one of
them turned around and nudged Jo to show him the
empty pirogue. All Jo said was, "Give me the glass."

As soon as Paloma was underwater she knew it was
the same manta, no question. But the wound looked ancient. The flesh had grown together—probably, Paloma
thought with pride, because I packed it so tightly and
took off the ragged pieces. All that remained were scars,
and an indentation behind the horn, and a crease where
the ropes had gouged deep into the flesh. There was no
blood, no seepage, and as Paloma stroked the animal
she saw that the abused flesh had even begun to
regenerate the protective mucus that covered the rest of
the body.

The manta lay perfectly quiet as Paloma's hands ex-
plored the injured horn, and against all her knowledge
and all of Jobim's reasoned arguments she began to
believe that the manta had returned, like a child
revisiting a doctor, to show Paloma how successful her
treatment had been. She knew it was stupid and impossible and not worthy of someone who respected the
sea, but she believed it nevertheless.

Her body triggered the first familiar alarms to send
her to the surface, and she resented them and dismissed
them and pretended she was a fish, until the second set

of alarms forced her to leave the manta. She looked down as she ascended, hoping the manta would remain until she could return, and because she did not look up she did not see that Jo had moved his boat. It now lay beside her pirogue, almost touching it.

She had taken a couple of breaths and cleared her mask before she felt the presence of the other boat and looked up and saw Jo standing in the bow of the motorboat, holding his harpoon.

"Bring him up," Jo said sharply.

"What?"

"Bring the devilfish up."

"What are you talking about? I can't bring him up."

"Yes you can. Do what you do and bring him up."

"I can't! But even if I could, why?"

"He has to weigh two tons. Good money."

"Money? For a *manta*?"

"A silver coin for every hundredweight. Cat food."

Paloma thought he was simply teasing her, insulting her for the amusement of his mates. "How would you get it home?"

"Tow it. You'll see."

"You're crazy."

"Bring it up!" Jo said. "Now!" He raised the harpoon over his head, threatening not Paloma so much, nor the manta ray, as in a gesture of defiance.

Paloma could feel, in her legs, movement in the water below. She looked down through her mask and saw that the manta was flexing its wings—not moving yet but about to. She felt a spasm of fear, for the manta could be about to come up on its own, and if it surfaced anywhere near Jo's boat—as sometimes they did out of playfulness or curiosity—Jo would surely plunge his harpoon into the animal and nothing she could do would help it.

The dart on the end of the harpoon was hinged: Moving forward, during the throw and as it sank into flesh, it would lie flush with the shaft of the harpoon itself. But when the harpooner set it, by pulling the shaft away and tugging on the rope, the dart would spring open into a horizontal, and where it had gained a smooth entry it would find no exit at all. The harder the rope was pulled, the firmer the dart was set.

The manta would never know what had happened.

It would have come to the surface unaware of danger and would have felt sudden, searing pain and would try to flee. Jo would give it line, would let it run, holding the rope just taut enough to keep the dart set and hurt the manta and tire it as it pulled the boat after it. Gradually, Jo would increase the pressure, hoping to make the manta bleed, which would tire it further, knowing that now every time the manta sounded deep the pain would be worse and so it would tend to stay near the surface.

After a while, the manta would stop its struggle and would lie exhausted on the surface, exploding in a brief flurry of panic only when the boat drew near. Little by little, Jo would pull in the line, and let it out again if the manta struggled, and pull it in again until finally the manta had no more fight. Then Jo would draw the boat right to the manta and would either beat it on the head with a club until he found its brain and stunned it so its gills could be slit and it would bleed to death, or he would find a way to tie a rope around the animal so it could be dragged backward through the water until it drowned.

If the manta came up on its own, it would be dead before this day was done.

Quickly Paloma hyperventilated, and Jo, thinking she was obeying him, instructed Manolo to hold his legs and steady him so that when the giant rose to the surface his throw would be true.

Paloma dived to the manta. It had raised its wings, and she could see the motion begin that would sweep the wings down again and drive the animal up, for it was angled upward, its head higher than its tail. She went directly to the horn on the right side, wrapping her arms around it and pressing down hard, willing even to cause it pain if that would make it roll down and away and free from people.

The animal stopped its rise and gently bent its head down and to the right, in perfect response to Paloma's hands. Together they began a graceful roll to the bottom.

Paloma felt something quick and sudden in the water, and she turned her head and saw Jo's harpoon hanging by its rope a foot from her head. Cast in fury and frustration, powered by the arm of one enraged, it had been driven six or eight feet into the water.

The thought flashed through her mind that a stronger arm might have struck her with the harpoon, and that thought was followed by the knowledge that a truly strong man would never have flung the harpoon.

The harpoon hung for a second, then was retrieved.

Paloma released her grip on the horn. The manta eased out of its roll and leveled off at a depth of perhaps a dozen feet. Still moving away from the boats, it started to rise. Paloma would have to breathe soon, so she did not try to stop the manta's ascent. If it rose to within a couple of feet of the surface, she could drop off there and dash up and gulp air and hope to return to the manta before it began a new loop toward the deep. She wanted to guide it as far away from the boats as she could, and then she would drop off for good and know that it was safe, for with his net down Jo could not haul his anchor and start his engine and give chase.

Paloma had one hand on the manta's upper lip and one on its wing, and her legs and feet flew free as the manta banked and dipped and soared, changing direction on apparent whim but coming closer and closer to the surface. Paloma had no idea where she was, but she felt sure that the animal had changed course so many times that it must have traveled far from the boats.

Then, as the surface swept closer and changed from a blue veil to the shimmering luster of wet glass, she saw the looming figure of Jo, standing in the bow of his boat, harpoon poised above his head.

The manta had brought Paloma back to where it had found her. It had let her guide it on a wide, eccentric circle, had changed direction at random, for in the memory of its brain there must be stored a signal that told it how to return her to where she belonged.

She lurched forward, tried to grab a horn and push it down and drive the manta under again, but it was too late. The manta broke through the surface, not in a jump but like a turtle coming up for air. And it kept flying, moving its wings just beneath the surface, carrying Paloma on its back, carrying her straight at the boats.

Looking over the hunch of the wing, along the horns, Paloma saw Jo as he for the first time saw that Paloma was riding on the back of the beast. His hands jerked and his eyes widened and he let out an involuntary shriek of surprise and took an involuntary step backward, forgetting that his legs were gripped by Manolo. He started to fall, determined to throw the harpoon, flung out his arms, let go the harpoon and sprawled on his back in the boat.

The harpoon arced up into the air, askew, and Paloma saw it strike the water butt-first and heard Jo howl in pain and rage, before the manta once more dipped its horns, as Paloma took a breath and together they dived beneath the surface of the sea.

They went under the boat. Paloma did not try to guide the manta, for she wanted it to go away on its own, and she would not try to turn it unless it seemed to be heading for the boats. She thought of dropping off, but sensed that it would come back for her, wherever she was.

The manta was going deep, almost straight down. Ahead of its wings Paloma saw two streaks, and she realized that they were not shafts of sunlight but the lines that connected Jo's boat to the net. The manta passed between the lines and continued straight down, toward what Paloma could now see as a misty hump near the top of the seamount—the net itself, surrounding a clot of hundreds, thousands of frantic fish.

If the manta did not see the net and turn, it would foul in the net and wound itself again, and perhaps foul Paloma in it as well, and if she became tangled she would surely drown. She tried to turn the manta, but it would not turn. It was flying as hard and as fast as it could, directly at the net.

It was in the last fraction of a second that Paloma knew that the manta did see the net, did know where it was going, knew what it was doing. The immense ball of trapped animals loomed out of the dusty fog, and just before chaos Paloma's mind took note of how vivid were the eyes of the desperate fish.

With a last thrust of its great wings the manta plunged forward into the net.

On the surface, in the boat, the fishermen stood ready for the manta to surface again. They scanned the sea, searching for telltale bubbles or swirls. In the bow, Indio had his hand on the anchor line, prepared to pull the anchor up; in the stern, Manolo's hand was on the starter cord of the motor. They could release their net and buoy it and leave it briefly if they had to, and they would if they were to harpoon the manta.

Amidships, Jo held the harpoon high.

"Holy Mother! Where are they?"

"She can't stay down this long."

"How do you know that?"

"Nobody can."

"What d'you mean by that?"

"I don't know. I just . . ."

"If you don't know, keep your mouth shut." Jo was annoyed at the awe in their voices. "She has big lungs, that's all."

"And she rides the devilfish into the deep. That's all. A lot you know."

"I said shut up!"

The talk took no more than a second or two, and during it Indio noticed that the anchor line was drawing taut, and by the time the talk was done the others had seen that the lines connected to the deep net were stretched and throwing droplets of water as the rope fibers trembled.

"Jesus!" Jo shouted, the only coherent word he was able to utter, and from then on there were only screams and shouts and cries for help.

The manta had driven on, into the middle of the mass of fish, until Paloma was engulfed in jacks. They were under her arms, down her back, between her legs, flapping through her trailing hair. They squirmed and gulped and defecated and shivered. The water roiled and clouded, but it made no difference because she could not have seen more than two inches in front of her even in clear water: All was fish.

Somewhere in the attic of her brain, alarms began to

sound, but another sentry in her head told her there was no point trying to obey the alarms: She could never make it from here to the surface in time.

The manta flew on, pumping its massive wings up and down, its horn protruding through the net, its head pressing against it. The net held, and strained, and the manta slowed for a moment.

Above, on the surface, the panicked fishermen felt their boat begin to move. The anchor had been pulled off the bottom and was dragging, and anchor and boat were being hauled through the water by the unseen creature that drove the net forward and down. And because the force was downward, the boat tipped and began to ship water; the fishermen didn't know what to do but bail, frantically.

Then the net burst. The manta had simply overpowered it. It burst first in the center, and the fish squirted out the hole like grease from a tube. But the manta did not squirt out; it flew on and pulled the connecting lines even tighter until, one by one, the fibers popped. One line snapped first, whipped the net around free at one end, releasing the manta to start for the surface with Paloma on its back and destroying the equilibrium of pull which was the only thing that had kept the boat steady above.

The change was not felt immediately, for the lines were long and it took time for the pressure to travel. But when the change came, it struck suddenly and without prelude. The bow of the boat, from which the first line had snapped, jumped out of the water and spun. Indio, who had been kneeling on a thwart, found himself kneeling on air as the boat shot out from under him. Then he fell onto his back in the water and sank until his violent thrashing returned him to the surface.

Seeing the bow fly up, Manolo had reached to steady

himself on the motor, but the stern had sunk and the motor he reached for wasn't there. He pitched overboard and somersaulted underwater and came up sputtering as the boat yawed away from him.

Jo was now alone in the boat, kneeling on knees bruised and bleeding, watching the sea with horrified eyes, wondering what next would erupt from the unknown below.

The manta flew for the surface, its wings pushing maelstroms that spun fish and blew sand and roiled water.

Paloma gripped lip and wing, but as the distant sunlight rushed toward her she knew she would not make it. All her alarms were in full cry—the pounding was thunderous in her head, the pain excruciating in her chest, her eyes seeing the light of safety as a pinpoint that expanded and contracted, expanded and contracted, as consciousness slipped from her.

The manta flew straight up, not this time to angle and glide but to fly free in the air.

Air was only a few yards away, now a few feet, a split-second in the flight time of the great animal rushing for the sun, when the switch went off and Paloma's brain shut down and she lost consciousness. All her muscles relaxed, including those in the fingers that held her grip on the manta ray, so she slid away as the broad plain of black back exploded from the water and launched itself high into the air.

It rose above the cringing Jo, higher and higher until it blocked the sun and cast a black shadow on the boat. Water flew from it all around and caught the light and shone in a corona that lit the edges of the ray, and Jo knew he was being besieged by a creature from hell. His lips moved in reflex prayer, his throat uttered guttural whimpers, and he threw his hands over his head to ward off doom.

The manta reached the height of its flight and for a moment hung in majesty against the brilliant sky. Then the heavier head and shoulders began to fall, leaving the tail where it was, and the giant embarked upon a graceful slow-motion back flip.

Jo saw it coming, and he screamed in fear of death, and fell overboard.

He splashed and sank, and even through several feet of water he could not block out the noise, the terminal, shattering crash as tons of cartilage and sinew came down upon the boat and disintegrated it.

The transom with the motor attached broke off and sank of its own weight. The rest of the hull, struck suddenly by such mighty force, splintered, and the splinters fluttered into the sky and rained down on Jo and on Paloma, who was floating on her back by her pirogue a dozen yards away.

The manta did not stop, was not stunned. It forced beneath the surface what few pieces of the boat remained and continued its roll down, backward, and away, then righted itself and shuddered and cruised slowly toward the sunlight again.

What woke Paloma was the lapping sound of the waves from the manta's splash against the wood of her pirogue. For a moment she didn't know where she was, and she grabbed her pirogue for safety. Before her and to the sides the sea was empty. Behind her, down-tide to the west, she could see nothing because of the blinding reflection of the sunlight on the water. She heard sounds that could have been voices, but they meant nothing to her; perhaps they were sounds fashioned by instruments in her own addled brain.

Her feet touched bottom, a hard, slick rock ledge near the island, and though she wasn't sure how she had gotten there so fast she was glad to be home.

Bottom? She shook her head and looked at the pirogue and at the horizon and at the softly rolling sea swells. She was in at least ten, maybe twenty, fathoms of water. Then what was she standing on? For, there was no question that she was standing on *some*thing. She drained water from her mask and put her face down and saw that the manta had come beneath her and had risen, like a balloon, until it rested just at her feet.

Did it want something? Was it injured again? Paloma took a breath and knelt on the manta's back, and, very slowly, it began to move. She stood, and the manta stopped. She knelt, and it started to move again; she stood, and again it stopped.

It's behaving like a dog, she thought; it's waiting for me. But that, she knew, was impossible; the animal didn't have such "higher" instincts. And she was reluctant to impute to it "higher" qualities as motives.

And yet she was impelled to respond, even if only to the appearance of a motive. So, disregarding the contradiction of all she knew or reasonably believed, she hyperventilated and dropped to her knees on the manta's back and gripped with her hands.

This time the manta did not start slowly—it dived fast, shooting for the bottom. Within a few seconds, the top of the seamount rose before Paloma's eyes. She expected the manta to slow and level off and cruise among the canyons, but it didn't. As it neared the upper rocks, it banked, like a fighter plane beginning a rollover dive, and aimed down the sheer side of the rock wall toward the blue mists.

Paloma's ears were popping, for she had never descended this fast or this far, and though she was nowhere near a crisis of oxygen, the strange new pressures in the strangely cold water made her pulse pound. She wanted to let go, but she didn't dare: She wasn't sure she could make it to the surface, however far it was.

At the edge of the darkness, down deep where there were no more reds or yellows or greens, where the blues looked indigo and the indigos violet and the violets black, the manta suddenly leveled out, banked sharply to the left, and entered a canyon in the wall of the seamount.

It slowed and stopped and hung above a sand bottom, its wings almost touching the rock sides of the canyon. Paloma looked up and could not see the surface—no sun, no shafts of light, just a vague lightening of the gray of the water—and a tic of panic shook her chest, the same kind of panic she felt when she looked down from a very high place. She lowered her eyes and told herself not to look up again, for there was no point: She would either go up with the manta, or she would not go up at all.

What was this place? Why had the manta come here? Perhaps it was to places like this that mantas came for refuge—deep, cool, away from the sun and the surface, protected by the canyon walls from the open-sea currents.

Below was sand, above was water, on the sides were walls of rock like any other rock, except . . . Something was strange about these rocks. They seemed to be themselves studded with countless small stones.

She wanted to get closer, to see more clearly this place she could never dive to on her own. She rose away from the manta, praying that it would not now suddenly decide to abandon her, and kicked quickly to one of the walls.

She reached out to touch one of the stones, and before her fingertips had made contact she knew what these strange walls were made of: Each of the stones was not a stone at all, but an oyster.

At first they had been unrecognizable to her because they were larger than any she had ever seen—out of reach of all fishermen, they had been allowed to mature completely—and because they were camouflaged—out of the sweep of the currents, they had been covered with living vegetation.

She reached immediately for her knife, but it was not there. She didn't stop to wonder why, or to search for it further, but instead she gripped an oyster with her hand and twisted and pulled until it came away from the rock face of the canyon.

Her fingertips were scratched and shredded, her palm bleeding from little cuts, but she felt no pain. Using both hands now, she grabbed and twisted and pulled the oysters free and stuffed them into her dress, dropping them down to her rope belt. When her front was full, she pushed the oysters around her sides to her back, not feeling the sharp shells slice her skin.

Finally, she fell off the wall, exhausted and aching for breath and stuffed fuller than a roasting chicken. She landed on the manta's back. Had it been a horse, she would have spurred it on, for she needed to go now, and in but one direction—up.

And the manta took her up, flying with the swift grace of a bird seeking the sky. Soon she saw sunlight and blue crystal.

At the last second, the manta slowed so it would not leap clear of the water, and like a whale it rolled through the surface and lay with its back in the air. And on its back lay Paloma, with her arms spread wide and blood running between her fingers.

The manta stayed with her until she had rested and swum to her pirogue and climbed aboard and emptied her dress of oysters. It stayed still as she knelt in the pirogue and watched it, silently, reverently.

And then, as the leading edge of the red swollen sun touched the horizon, the great ray flipped a wing and dipped its head and kicked its tail in the air, and was gone, leaving a ring of ripples that spread across the twilight water and were soon gone, too.

For a long time, until the sun had sunk and the sky had darkened and the first stars were faintly seen, Paloma continued to kneel in the pirogue, letting the tide take her.

Far away in the night, she heard the voices of Jo and Indio and Manolo, and the words she could discern across the still water were contentious and bitter and accusing, for now they were safely floating and no longer feared for their lives. Later, she would get a motorboat and retrieve them. She thought they would no longer be eager to return to the seamount.

The manta would not return, either. She felt certain of that, though she could not have said why she was certain. Perhaps it was part of having some of the good thing. Perhaps it was a feeling that nature had needed to restore a balance that had been set askew, and to restore it had used the manta ray and, to an extent, had used Paloma as well. And now that the balance had been restored, the manta was released to fly free.

But what did she mean by nature? What was . . .

She stopped thinking, and she looked at the spot in the sky where soon the moon would rise and hang like an amulet and cast its golden path on the water, and she smiled and said aloud, "Thank you."

ACKNOWLEDGMENTS

I am grateful to ABC's "The American Sportsman" and its producer, John Wilcox, under whose aegis I was introduced to the Sea of Cortez; to Stanton A. Waterman, for taking me along on the voyage and for his sage counsel and fine company; and to Susannah Waterman Becker whose inspired graphic eye captured the look of the Sea of Cortez.

P.B.